**Some kind of emotion flickered across her face so quickly he couldn't identify it. Anger? Fear? Or something else?**

"Did you see the man who drove that car?" he asked again.

A low rumble sounded from the direction of the bushes where Faye had emerged a few moments earlier.

Jake yanked out his gun and shoved Faye behind his back as he whirled around. Was the panther still out here, stalking them? Or was that more of a curse than a growl?

A full minute passed in silence. No more growls or curses. No rustling of leaves to indicate anything, or anyone, was there. He cautiously straightened and turned back to Faye.

She was gone.

So were her knife and her rifle.

# MISSING IN THE GLADES

## LENA DIAZ

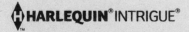

Thank you, Allison Lyons and Nalini Akolekar.
Thank you to my mom, Letha McAlister, who got such a kick out of this story. This book is dedicated to my friend and fellow suspense author Sarah Andre. Thank you for selflessly giving me your time, ideas and encouragement. This book would not have been written without you.

ISBN-13: 978-0-373-74928-7

Missing in the Glades

Copyright © 2015 by Lena Diaz

Recycling programs for this product may not exist in your area.

Printed in U.S.A.

**Lena Diaz** was born in Kentucky and has also lived in California, Louisiana and Florida, where she now resides with her husband and two children. Before becoming a romantic suspense author, she was a computer programmer. A former Romance Writers of America Golden Heart award finalist, she has won a prestigious Daphne du Maurier Award for excellence in mystery and suspense. To get the latest news about Lena, please visit her website, lenadiaz.com.

### Books by Lena Diaz

#### *Marshland Justice*

*Missing in the Glades*

### Harlequin Intrigue

*The Marshal's Witness*
*Explosive Attraction*
*Undercover Twin*
*Tennessee Takedown*
*The Bodyguard*

# CAST OF CHARACTERS

**Jake Young**—A police detective trying out his first case as a private investigator on the side, looking for a fresh start in Naples, Florida. But when his first major case takes him through Alligator Alley to the quirky town of Mystic Glades, he discovers a whole new world of danger.

**Faye Star**—This mysterious young woman sells her healing potions and mood stones by day and haunts the swamplands surrounding Mystic Glades by night. But when her secret past catches up to her, she may have to trust her life to the one man who could utterly destroy her.

**Calvin Gillette**—When this Naples man goes missing, he sets off a chain of events that threatens the lives of everyone who knows him.

**Dex Lassiter**—Founder and partner of Lassiter and Young Private Investigations. Is he trying to help, or does he want to keep Jake from digging up something Dex would rather stayed buried?

**Quinn Fugate**—This FBI special agent will do anything to close the murder case that mars his otherwise perfect record.

**Scott Holder**—Deputy with Collier County Sheriff's Office in Naples, Florida. Is his lack of interest in assisting Jake really a ploy to make him stop the investigation?

**Freddie Callahan**—Whiskey-loving owner and bartender of Callahan's Watering Hole, her drunken confessions provide Jake with a fountain of information. But is the information reliable, or a clever ruse?

# Chapter One

Jake aimed his pistol and flashlight through the chain-link wildlife fencing that marked where civilization ended and the Florida Everglades began. Behind him, his black Dodge Charger sat on the shoulder of a remote section of Interstate 75 that Floridians affectionately called Alligator Alley. With good reason. Alligators infested the swampy areas along this east-west corridor connecting Naples to Hialeah.

He swept his flashlight up and down the ditch behind him. Did alligator eyes reflect in the light? He sure hoped so. That might be the only way he'd see the hungry reptiles creeping up on him, looking for a late-night Jake-snack.

Not for the first time, he questioned his sanity in searching this dangerous area at night. But when a rare black panther had darted across the road in front of him and he'd skidded sideways to avoid it, he'd noticed a reflection in the beam of his headlights through the wildlife fence—a reflection that just might be the car Calvin Gillette was driving when he went missing three days ago.

In theory, if Gillette had crashed, the cable barrier system should have kept his car from sliding under the fence into the woods. And hitting one of the cables would have triggered strobe lights and an automatic notification to the Department of Transportation. But the system wasn't foolproof. A few months earlier a minivan hit a pole and went airborne, flipping over the cable without touching it and sliding under the fence into a canal. Jake figured if it happened once, it could happen again. And the few clues he had about Gillette's disappearance all led him to this same area.

A few minutes later, his search paid off. He found deep tire tracks in the wet grass. He hopped the ditch and pressed against the chain links—loose and floppy as they'd be if a car had hit the fence. Excitement sizzled through him. He stepped over the cable and slid through to the other side.

Grateful he'd worn boots for this search, he trudged across the damp ground to a thick stand of pine trees and palmetto bushes. Not anxious to go much farther in the dark, he braced his shoulder on one of the trees and used his flashlight to search for that elusive reflection of metal he thought he'd seen from the road. And suddenly, there it was, behind some bushes, too big and shiny to not be man-made. But without knowing for sure that it was a car, he didn't want to raise an alarm. Which meant he would have to go into the swamp.

It was times like this when he seriously wondered if he should move forward with his planned career change from police officer to private investigator. He was on leave from his police job to give the private sector a try, which was why he'd recently moved south to this unpredictable, dangerous, land-that-time-forgot section of his home state.

Tightening his hold on his pistol, he stepped past the line of pine and oak trees and—for the first time in his life—officially entered the Everglades. The difference in temperature struck him first. It was much cooler here, the musty, woodsy scent a welcome change from the thick humid air by the road. He'd expected the ground to be wet, slippery like the ditch by the fence. Instead, it was dry and springy beneath his boots, not all that different from the woods behind the house in Saint Augustine where he'd grown up, just a few blocks from the Atlantic Ocean. But where he'd come from he'd hear waves breaking against the sand, seagulls crying overhead. Here, the night was filled with the deep-throated bass of frogs, and a hissing noise that could have been either insects or cranky reptiles warning him to get out of their territory.

Keeping an eye out for panthers and gators and whatever else thrived in this foreign but starkly beautiful section of Collier County, he continued forward. When he rounded the clump of bushes where he'd seen the reflection, he discovered what he'd both expected and dreaded to find—a car, its dented roof, crumpled hood and crushed front bumper broadcasting the wild ride its driver had endured before the car slammed against an unforgiving tree.

The paint was scratched all to hell, but there was no mistaking the color or the make and model—a maroon Ford Taurus. A glance at the license plate confirmed it was Gillette's. The day he'd gone missing, it had been raining off and on for hours, which explained the dried mud caked on the half-buried tires. The ground must have been like wet cement when he'd crashed his car in here.

Fully expecting to see a body slumped over the wheel, Jake moved to the driver's door. But when he shined his light inside, he didn't see Calvin Gillette or anyone else. The car was empty. The now-deflated air bags must have saved the driver's life. If there'd been any footprints on the ground beside the car, they'd been scrubbed away by the rain and encroaching swamp before the heat of the past few days had wrestled the water back to its normal boundaries. So where was the driver? Had he gone looking for help and got lost?

He shoved his pistol into the holster on his belt to free his hands. In lieu of the gloves he'd have had if he were on active duty as a police officer, he yanked his shirt out of the waistband of his jeans. Keeping the cloth over his fingers, he opened the driver's door and grabbed the keys from the ignition. A moment later he popped the trunk. Except for a useless flat tire and some crumpled beer cans, it was empty.

Time to get the local police out here. He pulled out his cell phone as he peered through the driver's-side window, hoping to see some receipts or a map, anything to indicate where Gillette was headed before the crash.

*Bam!* The window exploded in a tinkling rain of glass. Jake dropped to the ground. A second bullet slammed into the door.

He cursed and scrambled around the front of the car, taking cover behind the wheel. He drew his gun again, aiming at the dark scrub brush and live oak trees where he'd seen the muzzle flash from the second shot. The moonlight cast deep shadows across the clearing, but he didn't try to grab his flashlight that had fallen on the ground. He wanted to draw the shooter out, but not by giving him a well-lit target.

"Police!" he yelled. "I can see you hiding behind that bush. Come out, hands up, or I'll shoot." He waited, crouched down, both hands gripping the gun. No sound. No movement. Half a minute went by.

Time to give his prey some incentive.

He aimed his pistol well above where the gunman had to be hiding and squeezed off a shot. It boomed through the clearing, hitting a small tree branch, sending a shower of leaves down to the forest floor.

"The next shot will be lower. And there are sixteen more rounds where that one came from."

Silence. Even the croaking frogs and hissing insects had gone quiet.

"Threatening to shoot me is a lousy way of thanking me," a voice called out, a distinctly *feminine* voice with a velvety Southern accent that had Jake raising his brows in surprise.

Had he stumbled across a beauty pageant queen in these woods? Or a debutante? He could easily picture the owner of that silky voice wearing a floor-length gown, sitting on a wraparound porch in the Carolinas, sipping a mint julep.

When the woman stepped out from behind the bushes, reality sucked the air from Jake's lungs. If there was such a thing as an *anti-*Southern belle, this astonishing creature was the physical embodiment of it.

Her curve-hugging blouse was Pepto-Bismol pink and was tucked into an equally pink collection of veils, or scarves, forming a semblance of a skirt that hung past her knees. Below the skirt was the only part of her outfit that wasn't pink—a pair of green camouflage combat boots. She was probably somewhere in her mid-twenties, and at least a foot shorter than Jake. Her waterfall of blond curls hung to her hips, sparkling like burnished gold in the moonlight filtering through the trees. A stray warm breeze lifted one of the gold locks and fluttered it against the muzzle of her rifle, which was pointed up at the dark sky overhead.

Jake pocketed his cell phone that had fallen by the tire before grabbing his flashlight and shining it on her. If she hadn't just tried to shoot him, he'd have been hard-pressed not to smile at the utterly adorable picture she presented.

He forced himself to focus on the fact that

she'd just shot at him. Twice. She was dangerous, at least while she was holding that rifle.

"Toss the weapon," he ordered.

"That's not a good idea. There are all kinds of dangers in these woods, especially at night."

"Now."

She let out a dramatic sigh and pitched the rifle onto the ground.

"Kick it away from you."

"Seriously? Do you know how expensive that gun is?"

He didn't bother to respond to that ridiculous statement.

She pursed her lips, not at all happy about his dictate. But she must have realized she didn't have a choice because she gave the gun a healthy kick. It slid across the pine needle-strewn forest floor and slammed against the car's rear tire.

Jake hopped to his feet and quickly closed the distance between them. "Who are you? Why did you shoot at me?"

She squinted and waved toward his flashlight. "Mind pointing that thing somewhere else?"

He relented and turned it just enough so it wasn't directly on her face.

She cocked her head, studying him. Her emerald green eyes were startlingly similar to the panther's eyes he'd seen reflected in his car's headlights earlier. Her outfit reminded him of the carnival gypsies he'd seen at local fairs, except for all the pink. Anyone else might have looked ridiculous in the flamboyant clothes. But, somehow, on her they looked…enchanting. If he'd seen her in a bar he'd be begging for her number and hoping to wind up sharing breakfast with her the next morning.

"Who *are* you?" he repeated, lowering his weapon. The little sprite certainly wasn't a threat to a man his size.

She braced her hands on her hips and tilted her head back to meet his gaze. "A local, which you obviously are not."

"That syrupy accent of yours doesn't make you sound like a local, either." He cocked his head, mirroring the same look she'd just given him. "But what makes you think *I'm* not a local?"

She snorted in a completely unladylike manner. It was hard for Jake not to grin and to maintain his serious look.

"Oh, please," she said. "You're oblivious to the dangers around here. You might as well wear a neon sign that says 'city slicker.'"

Her delightful accent was as intoxicating as her curvy figure. His fingers itched to slide around her tiny waist and pull her against him just to see how the two of them would fit. He gave himself a mental shake. Now was not the time to let his attention wander. He needed to focus. Finding this woman near Gillette's car couldn't be a coincidence. She must know something about what had happened. Maybe she'd even been a passenger in his car. That thought had Jake glancing around the clearing, his shoulders tensing. Was Gillette hiding in the trees, watching?

"Were you in that car when it crashed?" he asked. "Do you know the driver?"

She smiled as if she had a secret. "You said you were a cop. Show me your badge."

"My name is Jake Young. I don't have a badge because I'm not—"

She whirled around, kicking his feet out from under him so fast that he didn't have time to react. He landed on his backside, blinking up at the dark sky in shock. His flashlight rolled a few feet away, shining its light in a crazy arc. Before he could move, the little firebrand was on top of him holding the tip of a very large knife to his throat.

The last time anyone had gotten the drop on him had been…well, *never*. When the knife pricked his skin, his earlier amusement and distraction vanished in a flood of adrenaline and anger.

*The hell with this.*

He knocked the knife to the ground and rolled over in one swift movement, trapping her beneath him. Shackling both her wrists in one of his hands, he forced her arms above her head, using his body to pin her to the ground. But as soon as he felt her soft curves pressed to his and breathed in the flowery, feminine scent of her, he knew he'd made a tactical mistake. Especially when the breeze blew one of her silky curls against his face. *She* wasn't the one who was trapped. *He* was, trapped in a sensual hell of his own making. He silently cursed himself a dozen ways to Sunday.

*She just tried to shoot you. She's not your potential next girlfriend. Get a grip.*

"Let's start the introductions over," he growled, more angry with himself than her. "I'm Jake Young, from Lassiter and Young Private Investigations. And what I was trying to say earlier is that I don't have a badge with me because I'm on leave from my police detective job in Saint Augustine. I don't have jurisdiction around here. But that doesn't change who *you* are—the woman who's about to be arrested for attempted murder when I call the Collier County Sheriff's Office."

Her soft pink lips curved in an amused smile. "Oh, you think so, huh?"

"I know so."

In answer, she wiggled beneath him and tugged her arms, trying to free them.

A cold sweat broke out on his brow at his body's instant, unwelcome response to her sensual movements. He swore and shifted his weight, hoping she wouldn't notice her effect on him.

"Who are you?" he repeated between clenched teeth.

"Let me go and I'll tell you."

"So you can shoot at me again, or kick my feet out from under me, or stab me? I don't think so."

She huffed out a breath. "You're looking at this all wrong. I didn't shoot at *you*. And the only reason I knocked you down and pulled my knife was because I thought that you'd tricked me when you yelled 'police' and then said you didn't have a badge. What's a girl to think? I'm vulnerable, in a secluded area, with a stranger I believed was pretending to be a police officer. I have a right, a duty, to do whatever I can to protect myself."

He laughed without humor. "It's a little late to pull the helpless female act. Now *that's* a lie if I've ever heard one."

She beamed up at him as if he'd given her a compliment.

"Your name," he demanded.

"Like it really matters. My name is Faye Star."

Faye Star? He let the name sink in as he studied her more closely. "Miss or Mrs.?"

Her sinfully luscious lips curved in a suggestive smile. But her eyes were like a road sign flashing a warning, *danger ahead*.

"For you, it's definitely Miss," she purred.

He ruthlessly tamped down the inappropriate tingle of awareness that shot straight to his groin.

"Miss Star, for the last time, why did you try to shoot me?"

Her brows drew down as if he'd insulted her. "If I was *trying* to shoot you, you'd be dead right now. Like I said, I wasn't aiming at you."

"Right. How stupid of me to think you *were* aiming at me since you shot out the window and hit the side of the car where I was standing just seconds before."

"I shot *exactly* what I wanted to shoot."

"The car?" He didn't bother to mask the sarcasm in his tone.

"No, silly. The snake." She rolled her head to the side, angling her chin in an effort to point. "Over there."

He followed the direction she'd indicated. Lying under the driver's door of the car was the longest, fattest snake Jake had ever seen. Its head had been blown clean off. And its enormous body was sliced in half.

The breath hitched in his throat. He blinked in shock, again.

"That's a boa constrictor," she said, "in case you don't recognize it. It's not native to these parts but there are plenty of the buggers around. People dump them in the swamp after their *harmless* pets grow too big and eat the family dog. It was hanging on a branch above the car and dropped down when you were looking through the window. I saved your life. This is the part where you're supposed to apologize. And let go of my wrists. And get off me."

He shook his head, grudgingly admiring her skill with a gun. He'd have been hard-pressed to make those two shots himself if the snake really had been falling as she'd said. He climbed to his feet, pulling her up with him.

"You could have shouted a warning instead of almost shooting me."

"I told you, I always—"

"Hit what you aim at, yeah, got it. You still could have missed."

Her eyes flashed green fire.

"I'm going to release you," he said. "But

be warned. If you go for your knife it won't end well."

She glanced longingly at the thick, six-inch blade lying on the ground a few feet away. Where she'd hidden the thing he didn't even want to know.

She shrugged. "I'll get it later."

"Don't count on it." He let go of her wrists.

She frowned and tossed her long mane of hair out of her way, before crossing her arms beneath her generous breasts. "What are you doing out here?" she asked.

"Investigating the disappearance of the man who owns that car. And I'm the one asking questions. What are *you* doing out here? Since I don't see any cuts or bruises, I'm going to assume you weren't in that car when it crashed. But I didn't notice any other vehicles parked beside the highway, either."

"I live around here."

"For some reason that doesn't even surprise me. Where? In a tree house?"

Her eyes narrowed dangerously. "As a matter of fact, no." She fluttered her fingers over her shoulder, the moonlight glinting on the half-dozen rings she wore. "A few miles that way."

"Uh-huh. And you just happened to be wandering through the Everglades at ten o'clock at night."

She shrugged. "I couldn't sleep, so I went for a walk."

At his skeptical look she added, "A *long* walk."

"Of course you did." He retrieved his gun from where it had fallen when she'd kicked his legs out from under him and pulled his cell phone out again.

"What are you doing?" Her voice sharpened as if in alarm.

He gave her a curious glance. "Calling the police. Is that a problem?" He shoved his gun in the holster at his waist.

"It is if you're trying to have me arrested. I told you I wasn't shooting at you."

"Call me an idiot, but I believe you about that. I'm calling to report that I found Calvin Gillette's car. They'll need to process the scene and get some men out here to search for the driver."

Some kind of emotion flickered across her face, so quickly he couldn't identify it. Anger? Fear? Or something else?

"Did you see the man who drove that car?" he asked again.

A low rumble sounded from the direction

of the bushes where Faye had emerged a few moments earlier.

Jake yanked out his gun and shoved Faye behind his back as he whirled around. Was the panther still out here, stalking them? Or was that more of a curse than a growl? Was Gillette hiding in the trees, armed, ready to make sure Jake didn't make that call?

A full minute passed in silence. No more growls or curses. No rustling of leaves to indicate anything, or anyone, was there. He cautiously straightened and turned back to Faye.

She was gone.

So were her knife and her rifle.

*Damn it.*

He clenched his hand around his pistol. The one potential witness to whatever had happened to Calvin Gillette had just disappeared. She'd probably orchestrated that growl to distract him. Maybe she was a ventriloquist and a gypsy fairy all rolled into one.

The growl sounded again, closer, vibrating with malevolence.

Jake sprinted to the car, yanked the door open and jumped inside.

## Chapter Two

After notifying the Collier County Sheriff's Office about finding Gillette's car, Jake was told there weren't any available units to respond yet and that he should sit tight and guard the scene. He waited, sitting in Gillette's car, watching the woods in case the anticipated panther showed up. But the cat never appeared. Neither did the police. Had he known it would have taken all night, he would have gone home and gotten a much better night's rest than he had in the car—panther or no panther.

While waiting for the police, Jake had given in to the urge to search the car, carefully using his shirt as a glove. But he'd found nothing. He'd also called his client to update him on his progress.

By the time the police arrived and managed to cut through the chain link and get their teams into the clearing, the sun had been up for over three hours.

Jake shifted his weight against the pine tree behind him. The police wouldn't let him accompany them as they searched the woods for Gillette, so he was stuck here waiting, and watching the crime scene techs process the scene. But the hurried manner in which they were working had him clenching his jaw so tightly his teeth ached.

"Something bothering you, Mr. Young?" Scott Holder, the Collier County deputy in charge of the scene, said as he stopped beside him.

"It just seems as if your men are in an awful hurry."

Holder crossed his arms. "You're not from around here are you?"

*Really? This again?* Jake was tempted to check whether he was wearing a sign around his neck that said "Outsider." He shook his head. "No, I'm not from around here, not originally. I just moved from Saint Augustine a couple of months ago. Why?"

"If you knew this area, you'd understand how to interpret the signs."

So they were back to signs again. "Meaning?"

"Meaning, if you look at the branches that were broken along the path the car took to get in here, you'd see they're turning brown. They aren't freshly broken. This crash happened several days ago, probably the same day the driver went missing."

He seemed to be waiting for Jake to say something. "I understand what you're saying, but what's that got to do with processing the scene?"

Holder smiled the kind of tolerant smile one would give a toddler. "Any clues outside the car that could have helped us figure out where the driver went have been washed away in the heavy rains we've had. So there isn't much point in spending hours and hours scouring the mud. As for the car's interior, we'll process that back at the station. But I haven't seen anything that will help with the investigation. Where Gillette disappeared to is just as much a mystery now as it was when his friend reported him missing."

Jake still didn't agree with going so fast when processing a scene. But he bit back any further comments. He couldn't afford to make enemies of local law enforcement. His long-distance business partner, Dex Lassiter, wouldn't appreciate it if Jake's first big case in their joint venture damaged their chances of cooperation from the police on future cases.

Holder crossed his arms and braced his legs apart as he watched his men combing the ground beside the car for clues. "We looked for Gillette that first day and couldn't find head nor tail of him. And I certainly never expected he could have crashed out here without triggering the cable warning system. What led you to this location?"

"Incentive."

Holder raised a brow in question.

Jake smiled reluctantly. "I need to pay my rent, on both my apartment and my new business. The man who hired me to find Gillette is my first well-paying client. So, I've been busting my hump to figure out what happened. I interviewed dozens of people in Naples near his home and figured out that he'd driven down Alligator Alley the morning he disappeared. I became a pest at the rest areas asking commuters if they'd seen a maroon Ford Taurus the day he went missing. A handful of them thought they may have seen his car. I was able to narrow it down to a five-mile section of highway."

Holder had the grace to flush a light red. "Reckon we could have done the same, but our resources are limited with a heavy caseload. And it never occurred to me that he could have crashed his car out here without triggering the cable system."

Jake didn't bother to remind him that it had happened once before. He sympathized with

Holder's position. He knew all about budgets and manpower and prioritizing cases.

"I don't remember you telling me the name of the client who hired you," Holder said.

"That's because I didn't." And he didn't intend to. Quinn had been very specific about that. He didn't want to risk a leak that could spook Gillette if he somehow heard that the FBI was actively looking for him.

Holder's mouth tightened but he didn't press the issue.

Half an hour later, the CSI team finished its work, and the tow truck driver began the laborious job of winching the car out of the woods using the long cable attached to his truck parked on the shoulder of the highway.

Jake accompanied Deputy Holder to firmer ground and they both watched from beside Jake's Charger as the Taurus was hauled up the slope. Less than an hour later, the deputies who'd been searching the woods for Gillette emerged from the trees and climbed up on the shoulder to confer with Holder. Jake figured they'd found something, or were requesting more equipment. Instead, Holder clapped a few of them on the back and signaled to the DOT crew waiting by the fence. The workers immediately rolled the chain link into place and began refastening it to the poles.

"What's going on?" Jake asked.

Holder turned to him. "The search is over. They didn't find a trail, nothing to indicate where Gillette might have gone. They went all the way back to the marsh. We'll do some fly-overs in a helicopter, put out the word on the news, but there's nothing else we can do here."

Frustration had Jake's hands tightening into fists at his sides. Gillette was a seedy character who lived under the radar, taking odd jobs for cash. And he was rumored to be a petty thief in addition to the background Quinn had supplied. But that didn't mean he shouldn't get the same attention a more affluent or socially prominent person would receive in the same situation.

"I don't understand," Jake said, trying again. "You know he has to be around here somewhere. He couldn't have just vanished."

"If I thought there was any chance he was still alive, or that we could locate his body, I'd throw everything I had at him. But I don't, and none of my men do either."

Jake tamped down his anger. He didn't know this area, its dangers. Maybe Holder was right, even though everything about this felt wrong.

"Then what do you think happened to him?" Jake asked.

"The same thing that happens to anyone lost

out here this long—gators, snakes, other wild animals. More than likely his remains will never be found. We had a DC-9 crash into the Everglades just west of Miami years ago. Barely left a trace to show it had ever existed. You have to respect the environment around here and understand how it all works if you're going to thrive or survive."

There was no mistaking the hard glint in Holder's eyes, or his harsh undertone. The double meaning behind his words was clear. *Jake* needed to respect the Collier County Sheriff's Office if his *business* was going to thrive. Jake gave the deputy a curt nod, letting him know he got the message.

The remaining emergency vehicles and DOT truck headed out, leaving Jake and Holder alone on the shoulder beside their cars. What little traffic had backed up at this noonday hour was quickly getting back to normal.

"Did your team find anything useful that would at least explain why Gillette was driving east down Alligator Alley?" Jake asked.

"Not yet. My guys will process the evidence back in Naples, search his apartment again and interview a few more people. I'll also have some officers canvass the rest stops and recreational areas on I-75 for potential witnesses. If we find anything, I'll give you a call."

"What about the potential witness I already told you about, Faye Star? Are you going to interview her?" At Holder's exasperated look, Jake said, "I know you think Gillette's dead, but until I know for sure, I have to keep investigating. I think she might know something, or she saw something."

Holder let out a deep sigh. "Faye Star? Can't say I've ever heard of her. Did she give you an address?"

"Only a vague direction. She wasn't exactly cooperative. She waved her hand southwest and said she lived a few miles 'that way,'" Jake said. "Without a car she can't live far from here. She certainly didn't walk all the way from Naples. Are there any towns nearby?"

"Not really." He rubbed his jaw, looking hesitant. "I suppose you could try Mystic Glades."

Jake pulled out his cell phone and opened up a map on his screen. He typed in the name of the town, but nothing came up. "I'm not finding it. Mystic Glades you said?"

"You won't find it on any map. It's unincorporated, not even a real town. It's more like a collection of houses and a few businesses that just kind of popped up in the middle of the swamp. It was created using leftover buildings that housed construction workers when Alligator Alley was being built decades ago."

"Is it back toward Naples or the other way?"

"Other way. About ten miles east, around mile marker eighty-four."

"Ten miles? I don't think Miss Star would have hoofed it back that far at night in an area this dangerous."

Holder shrugged. "There's nothing else around here that I know of, although I suppose it's possible. You said she was uncooperative, didn't want to talk to you. Well, maybe she had an ATV. She could have pushed it until she was far enough away that you wouldn't hear the engine when she turned it on."

"Maybe so. But I'm still not sure where this Mystic Glades is located. I've been up and down this highway since yesterday morning. I don't remember a town close by, even an unincorporated one."

"It's a bit back from the road, sheltered in one of those tree islands in the saw grass marsh, right where it starts to get really wet and the cypress trees begin. There's a road, of sorts, leading off Alligator Alley to the town. Or so I hear." He fished his keys out of his pocket, seeming anxious to leave.

"What do you mean, 'so I hear'? You've never been there?"

"Nope. Got no reason to. I'll call you if we find anything on Gillette." He hurried to his car before Jake could ask him any more questions. If Jake didn't know better, he'd think the idea of going to Mystic Glades had Holder... scared. But that didn't make sense.

The deputy's tires kicked up dirt on the side of the road as he took off. He headed down the highway to make the turn toward Naples, leaving Jake alone, just like last night—minus Gillette's car. And minus the mysterious woman calling herself Faye Star.

He shook his head, thoroughly confused and aggravated over Holder's lack of interest in helping him. But searching the woods where Gillette's car was found, when the experts deemed it too dangerous, wasn't an option Jake wanted to pursue on his own. However, finding Faye Star was like a godsend, a bonus. He'd bet money that she knew more about the crash than she'd told him. And she just might be able to lead him to Gillette, assuming Gillette was still alive. Jake sure hoped so. He was acting as a pseudo-bounty hunter on this case. And if he couldn't produce Gillette, his fee would be cut in half.

A few minutes later he was driving toward mile marker eighty-four, searching for a road to a town that wasn't even a real town.

The traffic was light, but Jake still kept an eye out for other cars and trucks. Alligator

Alley was notorious for accidents. The eastern portion in Broward County was hemmed in by acres of saw grass that lured drivers into boredom and inattention. This western portion was just as monotonous, with its endless miles of pines bordering the highway, hiding the beauty of the marsh, canals and tree islands behind them.

But the deadliest ingredient to the crashes was the high speeds. Jake didn't want to become a statistic because some driver hitting the hundred-mile-per-hour mark didn't realize how slow Jake was going until they were on his bumper. For that reason, he pulled to the shoulder whenever he saw a fast-moving car coming up from the rear.

It took two passes and a full hour before he found the entrance to the nearly hidden road. It was where Holder had said, but so hidden he'd never have found it without specifically looking for it. And even though he was heading east, he had to make a sharp 180-degree turn right after a guardrail and drive parallel to the highway on a steep incline beside the wildlife fence to follow the road. It would have been the perfect spot for a speed trap, because no one up on the highway could see it down here.

When he reached a canal that ran beneath I-75, the dirt road turned the opposite way, directly toward the wildlife fence. As he neared the fence, it slid open to allow his car through. It must have had an electric sensor. But since it was right by the area where wildlife was funneled beneath the highway, it was unlikely any of the critters would have a reason to go near this section of the fence. The design of this little road seemed genius—almost completely hidden but still maintaining the integrity of the protective fences to keep drivers on the highway safe from wild animals running across the road.

About eight miles later he'd driven through several groves of oaks and pines, through a small raised section of road surrounded by saw grass, and then back into a thick tree island with bogs and marsh on both sides of the road. But he still hadn't located the illusive town. And for some reason the GPS map in his car was going nuts, its directional arrows blinking off and on. One moment it appeared he was traveling south, the next moment the GPS said he was going north. The crazy thing was completely useless. He tried punching up a map on his cell phone but there were no bars, no connection. He cursed and shoved it back in his pocket.

He was debating performing a three-point turn to head back to the highway when a black blur ran across the road in front of him. He skidded sideways, narrowly missing a panther—just like last night—and barely managing to keep his car from sliding into the marsh.

The wild cat bounded into the woods on the south side of the road, or at least, the direction Jake *thought* was south. Apparently the endangered panthers weren't quite as rare as they were alleged to be in this area. Either that, or the same animal was stalking him.

He shook his head at that fanciful thought and straightened his car out. He decided to give it a few more minutes before giving up and turning around, so he started forward again. He rounded a curve and slammed his brakes. The Charger shuddered to a stop. Ahead of him, a small, faded wooden sign shaped like an alligator declared the scattering of wooden buildings barely visible through the trees behind it as Mystic Glades.

But he didn't need the sign to tell him he'd arrived at his destination. Just like last night, a little pixie was standing there staring at him. She was in the middle of the road, in a breast-hugging lavender top, her lavender skirts flirting with the tops of her mud-caked combat boots.

And just like last night, she was pointing a rifle at him.

# Chapter Three

Faye couldn't believe her dumb luck and incredibly bad timing as she aimed the rifle at the grille of the black Dodge Charger. With the sun peeking through the trees behind her, she couldn't see the driver through the glare on the windshield. But she didn't need to. She'd seen that same car parked on the highway last night as she'd pushed Buddy's ATV along the edge of the trees. She knew exactly who it belonged to—the incredibly hot, but potentially dangerous cop playing at private investigator, Jake Young.

Pointing a gun at him wasn't the smartest decision she could have made. But as soon as she'd seen him rounding the curve she'd panicked. She'd tossed her purple backpack behind a tree and brought her rifle up. Now she had no choice but to "bravado" her way through this second meeting, and hope it was their last.

The engine cut off and the driver's door opened.

"You might as well crank that engine and go back where you came from." She tightened her fingers around the gun's stock. "This is private property."

"You own the whole town?" he quipped as he stood.

It took her several seconds to remember what they were talking about after she saw those broad shoulders again and those yummy muscular arms, that rock-hard-looking chest tapering to his narrow, powerful hips. *Yum.* Everything about him, from his dark, wavy hair to the boots he was sensible enough to wear out here, had her fighting not to drool. But now wasn't the right time for those kinds of thoughts. And without knowing *why* he was trying to find Calvin, it was too dangerous for her to even consider being his friend, much less anything more intimate.

*What a shame.*

She cleared her throat and hoped she hadn't stared long enough for him to realize what she'd been thinking.

"We're all family here in town, more or less," she said. "I speak for everyone when I tell you that you're not welcome." *Unfortunately.*

"I just want to talk. I need to ask you about

Calvin Gillette." He stepped out from behind the open door.

Faye almost whimpered. In the daylight, he looked even better than he had last night. Too bad she had to make him leave.

"I don't know who you're talking about," she said, trying to think of how to make him *want* to go. She debated shooting the car's radiator. But that would just disable it and give him an excuse to continue into town. And she really couldn't stomach shooting such a fine car. It was exactly the kind of car she'd have chosen if she could afford one, and if she had a driver's license. All shiny, glossy black with an engine that rumbled and purred like a well-fed cat.

"Now, why don't I believe you?" he said.

"Not my problem."

His boots crunched on the dirt-and-gravel road. She swung her rifle, following his progress.

"Stop right there," she ordered.

He continued as if he didn't think she'd really shoot.

Would she? Not normally. But desperate times...

She brought the rifle up to her shoulder and centered a bead on his chest.

He stopped about ten feet away, his eyes

narrowing. "How about pointing that thing somewhere else before one of us gets hurt."

"It's pointed right where I want it. I'm going to start counting. If you don't turn around and get back in your car by the time I reach five—"

He charged forward.

She was so surprised, she froze. He was almost on top of her before she swung the rifle a bit to the left and pulled the trigger, hoping to scare him into stopping.

*Bam!* The rifle cracked, barely missing him, just as she'd planned. But instead of stopping, he lunged forward and wrenched the gun out of her hands. He tossed it away and glared down at her, his dark eyes smoldering with fury.

"Give me one reason not to call the police to arrest you for shooting at me. Again," he demanded.

She craned her neck back to meet his gaze. "Because your cell phone probably won't work out here anyway?"

His eyes narrowed to a dangerous slit.

"Okay, okay." She held her hands up in a placating gesture. "Don't get so worked up. I wasn't shooting at you. I missed on purpose."

The skin across his jaw whitened beneath his tan. Obviously the man had no sense of humor and took things far too seriously.

"You're one of those ill-tempered Aries, aren't you?" she accused.

"Sagittarius," he snapped. "And just how is that relevant to you *shooting at me*?"

His declaration that he was a Sagittarius surprised some of the sting out of his insult that she'd ever miss something she aimed at. She automatically reached for the chain around her neck, but stopped before pulling it out. "No reason. None at all." She smoothed her hands down her skirts and tried to gauge his mood.

He took another step toward her, bringing them so close she could feel the delicious heat from his body. But her attraction to him was dwarfed by the formidable anger evident in every line in his body. He was as tense as a wound-up spring, ready to snap. And she was, unfortunately, the object of that anger.

If he were anyone else, she'd sweep his legs out from under him and go for her knife hidden in one of the many secret pockets in her skirt. But she realized two things at once. First, he didn't seem like the kind of man to fall for the same trick twice. And second, if she didn't hightail it out of here, right now, she might be in real trouble.

As if sensing she was about to flee, he grabbed for her. She ducked beneath his arms, taking advantage of their difference in height.

She ran as if a whole nest of hungry gators was after her.

He shouted some impressively colorful phrases and took off in pursuit, his boots pounding against the hard ground, his long strides rapidly eating up the distance between them. But she figured she had the advantage. He might be spitting mad, but she firmly believed her very survival was at stake, which made her feet fairly fly.

There was only one place of refuge with him so close: his car. She skidded around the open driver's door and jumped inside. She slammed it shut and punched the electric lock just as he reached her and yanked on the handle.

He leaned down, silently promising retribution as he glared at her through the window.

"Open. The. Door." His deep voice vibrated with anger, pounding through her skin like a hammer against a nail.

She shook her head, her long hair flying around her face. "Not a good idea."

"Now."

Did he think making his voice sound as if he wanted to tear her apart with his bare hands would make her more inclined to remove the only barrier between them? That was the problem with a Sagittarius—too unwilling and impatient to slow down and look beneath the surface to all the subtleties of a situation before jumping into action. Then again, sex with a Sagittarius lover, especially with a Libra—like her—could be explosive and make that overbearing nature superhot.

Counting on the fated attraction between their astrological signs to help her out, she aimed her most seductive smile at him.

If anything, his glare got worse. *Oh, dear.*

"Open the door, Miss Star."

"Not until you calm down." She added a contrite smile this time. But since being contrite wasn't in her nature, she wasn't sure she'd succeeded.

He stared at her for a good long while, as if he was considering all the different ways he could torture her before he killed her. Then he shoved his right hand into his jeans pocket. When he pulled his hand out, he dangled something in the air for her to see.

*Keys.*

*Shoot.* She hadn't even thought about starting the car or she'd have realized the keys weren't in the ignition. She tightened her fingers on the steering wheel, desperately considering her options. Jake Young didn't know her connection to Calvin or he'd have used her legal name instead of "Star." Which meant, he probably wasn't the man Calvin had called her about when he'd taken that disastrous, ill-fated trip down Alligator Alley on his way to Mystic Glades.

But if Jake wasn't someone from her and Calvin's past trying to find them, who was he working for? Had Calvin gotten into "new" trouble in Naples? Was that why someone was after him this time? It certainly was preferable to the alternative, and might mean that Jake wasn't a threat to *her*. Well, except for the part where he wanted to find Calvin, and she wasn't about to help him do that. And the part where she'd shot a gun around him several times now, and the stubborn man refused to understand she wasn't shooting *at* him.

Sunlight flashed off the keys in Jake's hand as he shook them out, making them jangle as if he were a prison guard about to take an inmate out for his last walk before his execution. Or *hers*. His lips curved in a feral smile. He pointed to the small black rectangle on his key chain—an electronic key fob.

Faye's breath hitched in her chest.

Jake poised his thumb over the unlock button.

She poised *her* finger over the lock button on the inside of the door.

They faced off like two duelers at dawn,

trigger fingers cocked and loaded, each waiting for the other to flinch.

*Click.* The door unlocked.

*Click.* Faye locked it again just as he grabbed the door handle.

*Click.*

*Click.*

*Click, click, click, click.*

His eyes narrowed.

She licked her lips, focusing on that damn thumb of his on the key fob.

*Click, thump.* He managed to unlock the door and lift the handle a split second before she pressed her button again.

*Game over.*

She scrambled over the middle console, cursing when her left knee slammed against the gearshift, sending a sharp jolt of pain down her leg. She fell on the slippery leather of the passenger seat, fumbling for the opposite door handle. She pulled it and shoved the door open.

"Oh no, you don't," he growled.

She felt, rather than saw, him lean inside to grab her from the driver's side. She pulled herself toward the opening and dived like a world champion. There was a tug against her waist, a ripping sound, and then she was free! She rolled out of the way a split second before he landed on the ground where she'd just been.

She was already splashing through the marsh, sprinting for the cover of trees, when she heard his bellow of rage behind her. It wasn't until she'd entered the much cooler air beneath the pines and knotty cypress, and felt the rush of air against her thighs, that she realized what her narrow escape had cost.

Her skirt.

JAKE STARED AT the surprisingly heavy handful of soft purple fabric in his hand. He supposed he should feel guilty. But once he'd recovered from his anger that Faye was getting away, he'd been too busy enjoying the view of her toned, gorgeous backside adorned in a lacy purple thong to do more than sag against his car and enjoy the show.

He shook his head in disgust. How had everything gotten so out of hand? He retrieved the rifle the half-naked pixie had pointed at him earlier, unloaded it and pitched the shells in the back floorboard of his car. Then he carried both the gun and the fluff of material to the tree line where she'd disappeared.

Taking devilish delight in knowing she'd have to spend hours cleaning it to make the gun usable again, he shoved the barrel of the rifle into the muck beside the road. With the butt of the gun standing up in the air, he was about to drape the skirt over the top when something heavy banged against the rifle. He felt along the fabric and found a hidden pocket, a deep pocket that contained the wicked-looking knife she'd threatened him with last night.

The evil-looking blade winked in the sunlight as if it were laughing at him. He carefully ran the rest of the fabric through his hands. But although he found more hidden pockets, they were empty. He draped the ruined skirt over the end of the rifle and added the knife to the rifle rounds in his floorboard.

He got back in his car and headed toward Mystic Glades again. He was just passing the alligator-shaped sign when he spotted something purple off to his left beside a tree. He braked and got out, drawing his pistol in case Faye had somehow managed to get past him to the other side of the road and had another gun hidden…somewhere.

When he reached the tree he discovered it wasn't Faye hiding there. It was a purple backpack that so perfectly matched the color of her outfit it had to be hers. He crouched down and rummaged inside, cataloging the contents: bottles of water, power bars, a towel, a first aid kit. Not the kind of supplies someone generally carried for a "walk." It was exactly the kind of supplies she might have if she were trying to find someone who'd gotten lost in the wilderness after a car wreck.

FAYE HAD RUN a good long way before she'd reached firm, dry ground. After finding a relatively clean-looking log, she perched on it to wait. She didn't know how long she sat there. But from watching the way the shadows moved, she figured it was at least an hour, long enough that Jake would have given up by now and gone back to Naples.

To be certain that he was gone, she'd have preferred to wait longer. But time was a luxury she didn't have. She couldn't afford to waste any daylight. Searching at night had proved far too dangerous, in more ways than one. So she wasn't going to do that again. But how could she search for Calvin if Jake Young was hanging around?

The battery on Calvin's phone had died yesterday while he was talking to her and he was hopelessly lost. He couldn't even give her any landmarks to help her find him. After surviving that horrendous crash, he'd foolishly headed *into* the woods instead of to the highway. His excuse was that he was afraid he was being followed, and he didn't want to risk being seen. But Faye wished he'd at least have waited until she got there. She could have found him that first night and she wouldn't have back-tracked last night to restart her search and run into Jake Young.

Her only comfort was that Calvin had packed supplies as she'd instructed—something she always encouraged anyone to do before venturing into the Everglades—and he had the basics he needed to survive. Well, assuming he didn't step on an alligator, of course. Or get bitten by a snake. Hopefully he'd heard enough of her own ventures in the 'Glades to know what to look out for. But no amount of book smarts could trump experience.

The sun was high in the sky now, about midday. She couldn't wait any longer, especially since she didn't have any weapons to protect herself out here. She was breaking all her own rules by being in the marsh without survival gear.

After a careful look around for predators, she jogged back toward the road. When she finally reached the archway over the entrance to Mystic Glades, she was relieved that the black Charger was gone. But discovering her ruined skirt fluttering in the breeze on top of her upside-down rifle, its nose shoved deep in the bog, had her cursing long and hard. If Jake were here right now she'd lob her knife, end over end, to bury itself in the dirt at his feet just for the pleasure of making him jump.

Wait, her knife. It had been in the skirt. She grabbed the fabric and groaned. It was far too light, which meant Jake had found—and taken—her knife. That was one more sin she could add to her growing list of grievances against the man, Sagittarius or not.

She tied the ragged edges of her skirt around her waist. It was a disaster, but at least it covered her bottom. It took three tugs of the rifle before the mud released it with a big sucking sound, making Faye stumble backward and re-igniting her anger.

A car rumbled up the road. Was Jake returning already? She rushed behind the nearest tree. The car came around the last curve and she relaxed. Not Jake. It was Freddie, probably with cases of moonshine in her trunk to stock up before Callahan's Watering Hole opened for business later tonight. Four more cars passed to and from Mystic Glades. Practically a rush hour for the amount of traffic that normally went up and down this road.

Most of the locals relied on swamp buggies for transportation and headed through the saw grass marsh behind town to barter and trade goods with others who lived the nomadic lifestyle. But it was occasionally necessary to make the long drive down Alligator Alley to bring back more substantial supplies, to exchange mail or even to go to a traditional job. Some of the town's inhabitants worked on the Gulf Coast in Naples. Others worked for the DOT, keeping the wildlife fencing and roads in good repair. Still others worked at the rest stops along I-75.

Faye did none of those things. She lived above the little shop she ran, The Moon and Star. Thankfully, with the orders she received from her catalog, she made enough money to pay Amy to help her part-time. Amy was at the shop right now. Faye didn't want to open herself up to questions about her state of undress. But she didn't have a choice.

She hadn't had a reason to bring her keys with her this morning, which meant she couldn't go in through the back door. She'd just have to keep to the trees so no one would see her until she reached the store. Then she could duck inside, make up some kind of story to placate Amy, and go upstairs to shower and change. After that, she could start another search. But first she needed to retrieve the backpack she'd hidden before Jake Young drove up.

After making sure no more cars were coming in or out of town, she raced to the other

side of the road. She reached for her backpack.
It wasn't there. She frowned. This was where
she'd tossed it, wasn't it? She turned in a slow
circle but didn't see the flash of purple anywhere. Instead, she saw muddy boot prints.
She hadn't misplaced her backpack.

*Jake Young took it.*

Cold dread snaked up her spine. Did he understand the significance of what she'd had in
that pack? He might be a greenhorn but he
didn't strike her as dumb. After finding her at
the crash site last night, and seeing the supplies
she had in her pack, he had to have connected
the dots. He had to know she'd lied and that
she was trying to find Calvin.

She pressed a shaky hand to her stomach.
Okay, no reason to panic. Not yet. Think this
through. All she knew for sure was that a private investigator was trying to find Calvin.
But he hadn't mentioned anything about finding *her*. If someone from Tuscaloosa had hired
him, they'd have wanted both her and Calvin, wouldn't they? But Jake hadn't tried to
grab her...or *kill* her. Which meant he didn't
know about her connection with Calvin, and
he wasn't sent by any of Genovese's associates.

So far, so good. That had to mean that whoever had hired Jake was from Naples. The
worst that could mean, unless Calvin had

done something really bad he hadn't admitted to since moving to this area, was that he'd skipped out on some debts. Maybe a finance company had hired Jake to deliver a summons to take him to court.

Okay, that would be bad, too. That would put Calvin in the public eye again, which would make it easy for their enemies to find him, and her. Shoot. No matter how she looked at this it was bad. There was only one thing left to do.

She looked at the archway over the entrance to Mystic Glades, sorrow heavy in her heart. This was her home, the only place that had ever felt like home. But from the moment she'd met Jake Young, this was no longer her sanctuary. It was no longer safe to stay, either for her or the people she loved. It was time to leave. Time to find a new place to hide.

# Chapter Four

Jake balanced his ladder-back chair against the wall behind him in the office of The Moon and Star, listening to his slightly inebriated new friend, Freddie, regale him with stories about a certain little golden-haired pixie. Since his latest run-in with Faye, when she'd nearly shot him—again—Jake didn't feel even a little guilty about the lies he'd told her friends. Both Freddie and Amy, the young girl taking care of customers out in the main part of the store, now believed Jake and Faye had dated in the past and that he was here to surprise her.

She'd be surprised all right, especially since his car was hidden behind the shop so she wouldn't know he was here until it was too late for her to avoid him.

Freddie—which Jake assumed was short for Fredericka—licked a drop of whiskey off her shockingly red lips and held the bottle up to top off Jake's already half-full shot glass.

He hurried to cover the glass with his hand. It was still too early for him to indulge in more than the few sips he'd taken to keep Freddie talking. And he needed to keep his wits about him for the inevitable confrontation coming up with Faye.

"Thanks, but I've had plenty."

Freddie shook her gray-streaked, faded orange hair in bewilderment and topped off her glass with more of the amber liquid. "No such thing as plenty when it comes to quality refreshment." She tossed the whiskey back in one swallow, her throat working and her eyes closing as she obviously enjoyed the burn. "Ain't nothing like Hennessey, my friend," she said when she opened her eyes. "I was saving that bottle for a special occasion. And this is definitely a special occasion, meetin' Faye's beau."

That formerly nonexistent guilt started niggling at Jake's conscience. He didn't want to go overboard with his fabrications and disappoint Freddie once she found out the truth. Apparently, in the thirteen months that Faye had rented this store and upstairs apartment from Freddie, she'd never once dated. Which seemed to make Freddie all the more eager to bring the two of them "back together."

"Now, Freddie," Jake said, "I didn't exactly

say I was her *beau*. I just said we used to be special friends back in high school."

For perhaps the dozenth time since she'd started tossing back shots, Freddie giggled. Jake didn't think he could ever get used to hearing that particular sound coming from a husky, bear of a woman who looked as if she could arm-wrestle just about any man and win—including Jake.

"I know what 'special friends' means," Freddie said, punctuating her statement with air quotes. "I had a few special friends back in my day. Why, when I wasn't much younger than you must be now, I had a *very* special friend, Johnny Green." She shook her head and finger-combed a strand of hair that had escaped her ponytail. Her faded blue eyes took on a faraway look as she began to describe, in lurid detail, exactly what she and Johnny used to do that was so special.

After a decade as a cop and being in all kinds of crazy situations, there wasn't much that could embarrass Jake. But he could feel his cheeks growing warm, listening to the graphic descriptions Freddie was using to describe things Jake really didn't want to hear about. Especially from a woman old enough to be his grandmother. He was about to beg her to stop when the bell over the front door rang.

*Saved by the bell. Thank God.*

The low hum of feminine voices told Jake that Amy and Faye were talking to each other. Amy was supposed to tell Faye that Freddie was in the back and needed to see her. That little twinge of guilt reared its ugly head again. Amy couldn't be a day more than eighteen and had been incredibly easy to fool with his lies. And here he was, corrupting her and getting her to lie, too.

There was probably a special place in hell waiting for him right now.

"Freddie, what are you doing back there?" Faye called out. "Is there a problem at the bar?"

"Nope, I'm just testing out my newest whiskey before I open tonight," she yelled back. As if to prove her point, she tipped her glass and drained it.

"I hope you haven't been waiting too long." Faye's boots clomped on the hardwood floor as she approached the back room. "You wouldn't believe the morning I've had so far. I tore my skirt, lost my knife, and my rifle is ruined. I had a run-in with a mean-tempered city slicker who doesn't know his ass from an alligator. It took a lot longer than I expected to get rid of—"

When she reached the doorway, her feet stopped faster than the rest of her. She had to grab the door frame to keep from pitching forward. She was still dressed in her lavender top. And her torn skirts were hanging provocatively low on her hips, held in place by two veils tied together. Her ever-present rifle was in her right hand, pointing up at the ceiling. The fact that she wasn't pointing it at Jake was probably only because she was too stunned to react. Or, more likely, she was worried it would backfire with all that dirt and mud crammed into the barrel, assuming she'd even managed to find more ammo after he'd unloaded it.

Not eager to test his theories around a trigger-happy woman like Faye, Jake dropped the front legs of his chair to the floor and grabbed the rifle out of her hand.

She blinked as if coming out of a daze and aimed a wounded look at her friend. "What is *he* doing here?"

"I think what you meant to ask," Jake teased as he set the muddy rifle in the corner, well out of her reach, "is why is Freddie drinking with a mean-tempered city slicker?"

Faye flushed a light red.

Freddie slammed her shot glass down and twisted around in her chair, looking behind her. "What city slicker? I don't cotton to none of them."

Jake grinned. Winning Freddie to his side

had been easy. Faye was proving to be a lot more challenging.

"I was just telling Freddie that I'm an old friend of yours," he said.

Faye's eyebrows shot up. "You are? I mean, you were? Telling Freddie that?"

He nodded. "I told her some of those old stories about our high school days in Mobile."

She went a little green. She had no way of knowing that Freddie was the one who'd told him where she'd gone to high school and that Jake still knew precious little about her.

"I also told Freddie how we planned on going to the University of Florida together but you ended up going to Florida State University instead. Funny thing is, I guess I got that wrong. Freddie said you didn't go to FSU."

Her face went from green to sickly pale. She glanced at Freddie, obviously wondering exactly how much she'd told Jake. "Um, no, no, I didn't. Freddie, can you give us a—"

"University of Alabama, wasn't that it?" Freddie wiped a trickle of whiskey from her chin, smearing her makeup like a brown streak of mud. "That's where you went to school, right? 'Cause that's where you and Amber met." Freddie smiled up at Jake. "Amber Callahan was my niece. She and Faye used to come here every summer between semesters. Seems like the whole town watched Faye growing up into the fine woman she's become. She and Amber both graduated from UA."

"Explains the accent." Jake lifted his glass in salute. "Roll Tide, roll." He downed his shot of whiskey in one quick swallow. The urge to cough and wheeze was overwhelming, making his eyes water. But he managed to cling to his dignity, just barely, and make it through the storm. Good grief the stuff was strong. He suspected the name on the bottle had nothing to do with the contents and prayed he wouldn't go blind drinking what had to be a homemade brew. It certainly wasn't Hennessey.

He cleared his throat and met Faye's look of impending doom with a smug smile.

"Faye, Faye," Amy yelled from the other room. "Sammie's in trouble out front. CeeCee has him wrapped up tight and it doesn't look like he has his alcohol with him."

Faye whirled around and ran down the hallway toward the front of the store.

Jake cursed and ran after her. CeeCee? Alcohol? He couldn't begin to imagine what he was about to see.

He caught a mind-numbing, lust-inducing view of Faye's gorgeous derriere as she raced out the door, her short, ruined skirt lifting up behind her before the door shut in his face. He yanked it open in time to see her pulling on the silver chain that hung around her neck. She lifted it out of her shirt and there were three small pouches hanging from it. She unsnapped the red one and dropped to her knees.

Right beside a man with an enormous snake wrapped around his neck and chest.

Ah, hell. Jake grabbed his gun and dropped to his knees beside her and a small group of people who'd gathered around the man being squeezed to death by the snake.

"Someone find the snake's head so I can shoot it without shooting this guy," Jake ordered.

"No," the man writhing in the street choked out. "No one kills CeeCee."

Everyone looked at Jake as if he'd just threatened to shoot a baby, or kick a dog.

Faye spilled the powdery contents of the red pouch into her hand. "Bubba, there's his head, against Sammie's throat. Grab it, hold it."

Two older men, probably both in their fifties, reached for the snake's head at the same time.

"Not you," Faye said, motioning to one of them. "The other Bubba."

The stronger-looking of the two grabbed the snake's head and forced it back away from Sammie.

"Hurry," Sammie whispered.

Faye leaned toward the snake.

Jake grabbed her around the waist, holding her back.

"I'm not letting you near that thing," he bit out. "It could kill you."

She gave him a surprised look. "I know what I'm doing. Let me go before CeeCee squeezes so hard Sammie has a heart attack."

He hesitated.

"Trust me," she said. "At least with this."

Since everyone was staring at him as if he were the devil, he reluctantly let her go.

She immediately slathered the red powder on the snake's nostrils and head. "Okay, everybody jump back. Bubba, release CeeCee."

Jake swung Faye up in his arms and backed away from the now violently twisting snake. Faye blinked up at him, confusion warring with some other emotion on her face.

"Catch him, Bubba," Sammie yelled. "I need to wash him off or he'll hurt himself."

Faye and Jake looked back at the street, but everyone had scattered. They were all running toward the trees between two of the buildings, including the man who'd had the constrictor wrapped around him just seconds earlier.

"I guess Sammie is okay." Faye laughed.

"This happens a lot around here?"

She grinned. "Often enough for me to always carry a pouch of snake repellant. I've told Sammie to keep some rubbing alcohol in his back pocket to use if CeeCee ever confuses him with food. It works almost as well as my repellant. But Sammie tends to forget."

Jake carried her into the store. "Sounds to me like he needs to let his pet go before it kills him."

"That pet is the only reason he gets up every day. It's what he lives for now that his wife is gone. He's all alone except for CeeCee."

He grunted noncommittally and headed down the hall.

Faye stiffened as he neared the staircase that led to her apartment. "You can put me down now. I'm not in any danger, not that I needed you to rescue me in the first place."

"You're welcome," he grumbled.

She rolled her eyes.

He started up the stairs.

Her eyes widened in panic. "Wait. What are you doing? Put me down."

He tightened his hold. "Not a chance. We need to talk. No guns. No knives. And no man-eating snakes. Just you, me and the truth."

## Chapter Five

Faye tensed in Jake's arms. She waited until he reached the top of the stairs and set her down to open her door. As soon as he let her go, she rushed inside and whirled around to shut and lock the door. He shoved his boot in the opening, blocking her efforts. There was no way to win against his superior strength, not in a direct confrontation without any tricks. She reluctantly stepped back and let him inside.

Her skirt slid dangerously low. She was forced to grab the tattered edges and retie the veils holding it together. Her face flushed as Jake's gaze followed the movement of her hands, lingering on her exposed tummy before sliding past the skirt to her naked thighs.

She'd flirted with him the first time she met him. But that had been so she could distract him and escape. Maybe he thought it was okay to stare at her like this because of how she'd acted last night. If he were anyone else, she'd have decked him already. But even though she was worried about his investigation, and what his presence here meant for her, she couldn't ignore the punch in her gut every time she looked at him. Attraction sizzled between them. Why did she have to be so turned on by a man whose very presence threatened her entire world?

She stepped back to put some much-needed distance between them, and so she could meet his gaze without craning her neck back at an uncomfortable angle. "How did you figure out where I lived? And how did you manage to turn my friends against me in just a few short hours?"

"Mystic Glades isn't exactly a big city. I drove down the main street and as soon as I saw a shop called The Moon and Star, I figured it had to be yours. When I pulled up front, Freddie came out of the bar across the street. I think she thought she was protecting you by asking me why I was there."

"Let me guess. That's when you lied and told her I was, what, your girlfriend?"

"I might have hinted at something like that. Freddie and Amy both thought the idea was sweet and helped me surprise you. Don't be mad at them."

"Oh, don't worry. *You're* the one I'm mad at,

not them. You might as well turn around right now and leave. You're trespassing."

In answer to her edict, he kicked the door closed behind him. He moved farther into the center of the tiny living room-kitchen combo. "You live here? Above the store?" He peeked into the guest bedroom that opened off the right side of the living room. It was empty, except for the twin bed and chest of drawers that had come with the place.

"Where I live isn't any of your business."

As if she hadn't spoken, he crossed to the left side of the living room to *her* bedroom and went inside. He flicked the ballerina-pink comforter on her bed before examining the collection of figurines on her dresser. When he picked up the centaur holding a set of scales, she marched forward and plucked it out of his hand. Had she really found him appealing a minute earlier? She never could stand a bully. And she resented him forcing his way into her private sanctuary. She carefully set the figurine back on the dresser.

"Get out," she ordered.

His smile disappeared in a flash. The cold look that replaced it had her shivering inside and wondering if his earlier smile had been a ruse to make her let down her guard. It would certainly explain how he'd gotten past

Freddie's prickly exterior. She couldn't believe it when she'd found her friend drinking with Jake as if they were old buddies.

"Get out, or what?" he said. "You'll call the police? I know I can get service here. I did earlier, down in your office, when I was surfing the internet." He pulled his cell phone out of his jeans pocket and held it out to her. "Be my guest. After they get here, I'll tell them to search their databases for Faye Star. How long do you think it will take them to figure out that Faye Star doesn't exist? And how long before they get curious to find out *why* she doesn't exist?"

The blood rushed from her face, leaving her cold. "That's crazy."

"Is it? I can't find your name in any official databases, not here in Florida." He arched a brow. "Of course, I haven't checked Alabama yet. Maybe I need to surf the web a little more."

Her fingernails bit into her palms. "What do you want from me?"

He stepped closer, crowding her back against the dresser. "I want the truth."

Faye reached her right hand behind her, quietly pulling one of the drawers open a crack to grab the knife inside. "What truth?" she said, stalling for time. "You're looking for the guy who drove that car, right? Well, I don't know where he is. That's the truth."

"I don't believe you."

"I don't care." She fumbled behind her in the drawer.

Jake cocked his head. "What's wrong, Faye? Can't find your knife?"

She stilled and dropped her hand to her side. "What did you do, search my apartment before I got here?"

"You'd better believe I did. Self-preservation. I've learned never to underestimate you. It was easy getting Freddie to let me up here. I just told her I needed to use the bathroom."

They faced each other like two boxing opponents, each waiting for the other to make the first move. But Faye knew that fighting him wasn't an option, not without a weapon and a clear avenue of escape. Even if she managed to drop him to the floor, she wouldn't have any way to get past him and out the door. The bedroom was too small. All he'd have to do was reach out and grab her as she jumped over him to get away. She chewed her bottom lip in indecision.

Jake's anger seemed to evaporate as he looked down at her. "I know you're hiding from something, or someone. That's easy to figure out. But I'm not here to expose your secrets or dig into your past. I'm here for one reason, to find Calvin Gillette. And I believe you're the key to finding him. If you'll talk to me, and help me, I promise I won't do anything that will jeopardize your life here. I won't tell anyone where you are." He smoothed her hair out of her eyes, then placed his hand on her shoulder and gently squeezed. "Help me, Faye. Please."

It was so tempting to believe him, to believe the gentleness of his touch, the plaintive appeal in his words. She would love to trust him, ease her own burden by letting him share it. She needed to find Calvin, too. Was it possible Jake wasn't really a threat? That would mean she didn't have to leave Mystic Glades, leave her friends.

"Who are you working for?" she asked. "What does he want with… Gillette?"

"I can't tell you that."

"Does he want to harm him?"

Jake's jaw tightened. "I'm not in the business of finding people and turning them over to someone who's going to hurt them. The answer to that insulting question is a definite 'no.'"

His defensiveness seemed genuine. Maybe the client who'd hired Jake was a friend of Calvin's trying to find him for some reason she didn't know about. Maybe Calvin had overreacted and had gone on the run thinking he was in trouble when he really wasn't.

"What makes you think I know this Gillette guy? Or that I can help you find him?" she asked, trying to sound nonchalant.

He dropped his hand to his side. For some reason, the disappointment on his face sent a stab of guilt straight to her heart.

"I found the backpack. You were searching for him this morning, just like last night. Can we skip past the lies now?"

"What makes you think it's my backpack?"

His mouth tightened into a firm line.

"Okay, okay." There was no point in denying this particular accusation. If he'd searched her apartment for weapons then he'd probably noticed a few other things, such as that she had the same style of backpack in her closet in many different colors to match her other outfits. And that the bottled water and power bars in the purple backpack were the same brands as the ones in her pantry. She tried to bluff her way into a new explanation.

"I admit it. The backpack is mine. But only because I found that car a few days ago and realized the driver was probably hurt and wandering the woods and needed help. I've been searching for him, to help him, not because I know him."

"I think you can come up with a better lie than that."

"I'm not lying."

"Right. You were concerned for a stranger, so concerned you've spent the past few days searching for him. But you weren't concerned enough to call the police or to tell any of your friends here in town so they could help you find him. Try again."

She crossed her arms. "Why are you trying to find this guy? Who hired you?"

He seemed to consider that question, then nodded as if he'd decided it was okay to tell her. "My client is Quinn Fugate. He's Calvin's brother, different fathers, different last names. He only found out recently that they were related and is trying to connect with him. He'd tracked Calvin down through another investigator to Naples. But a friend of Calvin's reported him missing before Quinn could hop on a plane and go see him. The police gave up searching for Calvin after the first day. That's why Quinn hired me. And that's why I need to find Gillette before he dies out in the swamp. I'm here to help Gillette. That's all. Nothing more."

Hope had her staring into his eyes, trying to gauge the truthfulness of his words. He *looked* as if he was telling the truth. His story sounded plausible. And the name Quinn Fugate meant nothing to her, which was a relief. It *was* possible Jake was telling the truth. She honestly didn't know if Calvin had a brother or not. Based on their shared past, it was entirely possible. And right now, there was no way to ask him. But wouldn't it be wonderful if Calvin had a family he'd never known about, a family that wanted him after he'd been alone for so long?

*Was* Jake telling the truth? He certainly looked sincere, and he sounded sincere. What if he was lying? What if he wanted to use her to find Calvin? She could try to shake him, continue her search alone. But that wouldn't stop him. He'd be out searching, too. Maybe he'd even bring others to help. That would make it even worse for Calvin, to have more people looking for him.

So what were her choices? Search alone—assuming she could manage to get away without Jake following her. Or combine their resources, search together. That way she could keep an eye on him. Wasn't that better than knowing he was out there somewhere, but not knowing where? What was that saying, keep your friends close, your enemies closer?

"Faye?" He watched her intently, waiting for her decision.

"You want me to help you find this guy, the one who was driving the car?"

"Calvin Gillette, yes." He sounded disappointed again that she wouldn't admit she knew him. "You said you were worried about him, a *stranger* out in the 'Glades, and you wanted to help him. Together we might do better than either of us is doing apart. You can take me around town to ask some questions, see if anyone has seen Gillette. That might narrow down our search area. Once I find him, I deliver the information about his brother. Then it's up to him whether to pursue it or not. My job is over at that point."

"You won't tell anyone outside of Mystic Glades that I live here?" she asked.

He pressed his hand to his heart. "As long as you don't try to shoot me again, I have no reason to tell anyone about you."

She put her hand on top of his, feeling his pulse leap beneath her fingers.

He cleared his throat. "Um, what are you doing?"

"I'm trying to read your spirit, see what kind of man you are inside."

He opened his mouth to say something.

"Be quiet."

His brows rose but he didn't say anything. She closed her eyes, leaning toward him, feeling his warmth flow through her. Reading people, knowing their true nature, was something she'd always had an instinct for. She didn't know if it was a sixth sense, or just that she paid more attention than most people. But as long as she could touch someone, and listen to the way their body attuned itself to hers, she'd always believed she could read the good inside them.

A sense of calm flowed over her. She smiled as she opened her eyes. "You're a good man, Jake Young. I can feel it inside you."

His eyes widened. "You can?"

"Yes, I can. And I trust you. I'll help you find Calvin."

"Calvin? Not Gillette this time?"

She shook her head. "No. I still have my secrets, but I admit that I know him. And I want to find him, before something bad happens out in the swamp. We'll work together. Deal?" She held out her hand.

He hesitated, but finally took her hand in his and shook it. "Deal."

That increasingly familiar tingle of awareness shot through her. She tugged her hand from his and waved at her torn clothes, the smears of dirt on her arms. "I need to shower and change. And then I think we should sit down and plan our search. I've spent days going in circles without any success. I'd rather lose the rest of the daylight we have today figuring out a plan than searching for a few hours and coming up with nothing again."

She waved her hand toward her bedroom doorway. "You can set up in the guest room for tonight. If you don't have extra clothes I can borrow—"

"I always keep a go-bag in the trunk of my car. I'll run down and get it. It's got everything I'll need."

JAKE PITCHED HIS go-bag on the ground and slammed his trunk. He uttered a few choice curse words and leaned back against his car, guilt riding him like a double-edged sword. He'd done what he came here to do. His job. He'd somehow, inexplicably, gained Faye's trust. But instead of feeling a sense of accomplishment, he was drowning in a sense of betrayal.

How could she just touch him and decide he was a "good" man? Why the hell would she trust him so completely after just meeting him? How she'd managed to survive this long with such a naive way of looking at the world around her was beyond him. The woman needed someone to watch out for her, to protect her from the evil in the world.

And to protect her from men like him.

He shook his head in disgust. He'd moved to Naples for a fresh start, and here he was about to hurt someone all over again. If there was some way to go back in time and not take this case, he would have. But he'd signed a contract, accepted the money. And even though he hated what he was about to do to Faye, it *was* the right thing to do. He just hated that he was the one doing it.

He grabbed his bag and went back upstairs. The shower was still running. Faye's soft voice sang some kind of tune he'd never heard before. He'd half expected her to have disappeared again by the time he'd come back inside. And part of him had wished she had.

*Enough.* He did have a job to do. It was time he did it. Although he'd already performed a cursory search earlier when he'd used the bathroom excuse to go up to her apartment, he performed a more thorough search now. He snooped in every drawer, every closet, even beneath the cushions on the small couch and chair in the main room.

The little pixie wasn't much for keeping things neat and tidy. Her belongings seemed to occupy whatever space they happened to land in when she was finished with them. But the kitchen was spotless, the small bathroom off the guest room shiny and smelling like fresh lemons. At least there weren't any more weapons hiding anywhere, unless they were in her bedroom and he hadn't found them earlier. He'd have to be careful until he had a chance to more thoroughly search that room.

Pausing by her bedroom door again, he listened, assuring himself she was still in the shower. He crossed to the couch and plopped down to make a quick call.

"Special Agent Quinn Fugate," the voice on the line answered. Static reminded Jake of the unreliableness of cell phones around here.

"Quinn, it's Jake Young."

"Hold on."

Jake heard office sounds: ringing phones, people talking. Then a door closed and the sounds faded away.

"Sorry about that. We've got a bad connection and it's too noisy to hear you in the other room," Quinn said. "Go ahead. Have you found Gillette?"

He chose his words carefully, not willing to paint himself into a corner if things didn't go as planned.

"Not yet, but I have a good lead. I'm convinced he was on his way to a town called Mystic Glades when he crashed his car."

"Mystic Glades? Never heard of it."

The bathroom shower shut off. Jake lowered his voice to barely above a whisper. "It's about eight miles south of mile marker eighty-four on Alligator Alley, the stretch of I-75 that runs across the lower part of the state from the Gulf Coast to the Atlantic."

The door to the bedroom opened. Faye stepped out wearing a pink terry-cloth robe that would have been conservative except that it barely came to the tops of her thighs. His pulse slammed in his veins just thinking about what she might be wearing underneath—or *not* wearing. But the suspicious look she gave him as he held the phone had him rushing to cover his tracks.

"Got to go, Mom," Jake said. "Call you later."

## Chapter Six

Jake had to quicken his stride the next morning to catch up to Faye as she hurried down the stairs to the store. She might have agreed to work with him to find Gillette, but she obviously wasn't planning on making it easy. He didn't mind so much if it meant she'd sashay that gorgeous rear of hers in front of him in tight jeans. Her mouthwatering chest was cupped in an equally tight, green lace top that had him struggling to meet her gaze whenever she was facing him. Today was going to be a study in both pleasure and torture at the same time.

They'd gone over a crude map last night, marking off the areas she'd already searched. He'd shown her how to mark off the areas in a grid pattern to make the search more efficient. She'd seemed grudgingly impressed. But before they searched anywhere, they were going to talk to some townspeople as he'd suggested, and see if anyone had seen Gillette. Faye hadn't wanted to let anyone know about him, but she understood that time was of the essence now, and if someone could help narrow down the search area, that increased the odds of finding him alive.

Jake followed her through the short hallway toward the main room that made up the store. But as they passed the office they'd been in yesterday, she turned around and pulled him inside. She closed the door. The click of the lock had Jake's brows rising.

"What are you doing?" he asked, wondering if she'd maybe changed her mind about helping him with the search.

"We need to decide how we're going to play this." She placed her hand on his chest.

His pulse immediately sped up. He took a wary step back, forcing her to drop her hand. "What do you mean?"

She closed the distance between them again. "Yesterday you told Freddie and Amy that you and I had a past...a relationship. I actually think that's a good idea. If we keep up that ruse, people here will be more inclined to talk to you, to answer your questions."

His mouth went dry. "You want to pretend we're, what, lovers?"

"Is it really that far-fetched? We're obviously

both attracted to each other. It wouldn't be a stretch to convince people we're lovers, at least not on my part." She ran her fingers down his chest and hooked them in the top of his jeans.

He stumbled back until the wall stopped him from backing up any more. Faye smiled and stalked forward until her breasts were pressed against him.

"What's wrong, Jake?"

"I, uh, we don't know each other that well. I don't think this is a good idea." He clamped his mouth shut. Good grief. He sounded like a girl. His words rang false, too, since all he wanted to do was grab her and crush her against him. He tried, really hard, not to let his gaze dip to the cleavage pressed against his ribs.

He failed miserably.

She smoothed her fingers up the side of his neck to play with his hair. He shuddered before he could stop himself.

"We'll have to come up with a story about how we met," she said. "Something not too complicated so we don't get tripped up on the details, right?"

Making up a cover story. Now this was something he could do. He grabbed on to her suggestion like a drowning man grabbing a life preserver. "When Freddie told me you went to high school in Mobile, I told her I went there, too. So we'll have to stick to that."

"Hmm. Maybe. Where *did* you go to high school?" she asked.

"Nease. It's in north Saint Johns County, right outside of Saint Augustine." What the hell was she doing to the back of his neck? Her fingers were drawing little circles that shot heat straight to his groin.

Her eyes lit up. "Nease? Did you know Tim Tebow? The football player? He went there, right?"

Irritation flashed through him. What was it about women and Tim Tebow?

"Never met him. I graduated quite a few years before he came on the scene."

"Bummer." She chewed her bottom lip. "*Quite* a few years, huh? Just how old are you?"

"Why?"

"Because we're trying to pretend we went to school at the same time. I don't think we can pass for having been in high school together, unless you got held back a few years. How about college? People go there at all different ages. I graduated just a few years ago. How long ago did you graduate? Or did you even go?"

He narrowed his eyes. "Yes, I went to college. And yes, I graduated. But you do have a point about the age difference. I didn't think about that when I told Freddie we both went to high school in Mobile."

Faye waved her hand in the air—unfortunately, not the one that was doing sinful things to the back of his neck. If she didn't stop soon he might set back civilization thousands of years and throw her over his shoulder like a caveman.

"Don't worry about it," she said. "I doubt Freddie remembers much about the conversation. She was well into the brew by the time I got here yesterday."

He pulled her hand down and captured it against his chest out of desperation. "Okay. So we met in college. I was a senior who started a little late, if anyone asks. And you were a freshman. Will that work? University of Alabama, right? In Tuscaloosa?"

Her smile faded. "Just how much do you know about me?"

"Not nearly enough. Just what I tricked out of Freddie. What did you study in college?"

She looked as if she was still wondering what all Freddie might have told him, but she answered anyway. "Biology, with a focus on ecology and plant and animal studies."

"I suppose that makes sense."

She frowned. "What's that supposed to mean?"

"Just that you seem so at home outdoors. It makes sense you would have studied plants and ecology."

"What about you? I'm guessing something like exercise science. I can totally see you as a trainer at a gym, or with a professional football team."

This time it was his turn to frown. "Because?"

She waved her free hand toward him. "Look at you. Six foot, what—one, two? With muscles...everywhere. You were probably a quarterback, right?"

He rolled his eyes. "No, I wasn't. I didn't play football. And I studied criminal justice. Now there's just one more little detail we need to take care of."

He put his hands on her shoulders, intent on pushing her away. Instead, she slid both her arms up around his neck and locked them together. "Jake, quit fighting this...thing between us."

"We're...working together. We should keep it professional."

This time it was her turn to roll her eyes. "If we're going to say we're lovers, we have to be comfortable kissing, right? To be convincing? If you won't kiss me, I can't help you."

His gaze dropped to her lips. "So, this is part of our…professional relationship then?"

"Sure. Whatever. Just hurry up and kiss me."

His last shred of resolve to do the right thing snapped like a tattered thread. He swooped down and covered her mouth with his. Her mouth opened and she deepened the kiss, taking it from warm to molten in the space of a breath. She pulled him closer, standing on tiptoe, pressing her soft breasts against him as her tongue tangled with his. Heat raced across every nerve ending in his body, numbing his brain to logical thought.

He slid his hand over the curve of her bottom, lifting her up off the floor, fitting her softness to his hardness. She moaned deep in her throat, demanding more, feathering her hands through his hair. She lifted her legs and wrapped them around his waist.

The shocking heat of her against him made him stumble. He cursed against her mouth. She laughed and kissed him again. He turned and pressed her against the wall, ravenous for the honeyed taste of her, the sweetness of her surrender, the savageness of her response. He drank in her every touch, every sexy little moan, every seductive slide of her body against his.

Her hair swept across his hand on her bottom, teasing him with its velvety softness, curling around his fingers. An erotic image of that beautiful hair sweeping over his naked body had him tightening painfully against her.

A bed. He had to find a bed. Or maybe the desk would work. He couldn't wait long enough to find a bed. He had to have her now. He whirled around and sat her on the desk, standing between her legs, breaking the kiss just long enough to reach for her shirt to pull it up over her head.

But she wouldn't let him. She was too busy fumbling with his belt buckle, trying to unfasten it. He looked down at her fingers working his belt loose, and that brief moment of lost contact between them was just enough for the haze of lust to allow his brain to switch back on. What was he doing? This was crazy, wrong on so many levels. She trusted him, and he was betraying her with every breath he took. He couldn't cross this one last line. Once she found out the truth about him, she'd hate him forever. And he'd deserve it. He had to put a stop to this, even if it killed him.

He grabbed her hands and trapped them between his.

She looked up at him in question.

"We have to stop," he whispered, barely able to force his voice past his tight throat. "You deserve better than this, a quickie in a back-room office. Amy could discover us at any moment. And we should be out there trying to find Gillette."

She blinked as if just realizing where they were, what they were doing. The fog of passion in her eyes dimmed and she dropped her hands. Her face flushed with heat, but instead of withdrawing or shoving him away, she grinned. "Wow. That was...hot."

He laughed and pressed his forehead against hers. "You're like a breath of fresh air, you know that? And way hotter than hot."

"Yeah, I know. It's the hair, isn't it?" she teased, as she refastened his belt.

In spite of his renewed good intentions, he couldn't resist running his hands over the silky mass. "Trust me. The entire package is sexy as hell, with or without your gorgeous hair."

She grinned, apparently liking that. "Well, thanks for stopping. I guess. Because I sure wasn't going to. But you're right. The desk isn't exactly comfortable. Next time, we might want to plan the location better." She gave him an outrageous wink and shoved him back so she could hop down from the desk.

"I've got to check with Amy about her schedule and make sure she can cover the shop."

And just like that, she was gone.

It took Jake several more minutes before his breath returned to normal and he was capable of walking again. Together, he and Faye were like a torch and gasoline—he wasn't sure which one was which. All he knew was that he had to keep his hands off her. He couldn't risk something like this happening again. Which meant the next few hours, or days, were going to be sheer hell.

A few minutes later, with his libido safely under control again—or so he hoped—he left the office and entered the main shop. He hadn't paid much attention to the store yesterday. But since Faye was on the other side of the room talking to Amy, he took a look around. It was one large rectangular room, with deep, plush royal blue carpet on the floor. Matching blue walls contrasted against the bright white molding on the large picture windows on each side of the door. A long counter ran along the back right side of the store. There wasn't a cash register anywhere that he could see, but Amy seemed to have taken up residence behind the counter, so that was probably where people would make their purchases.

Amy gave him a friendly wave. He returned her wave and crossed to the left side of the store to wait by one of the big windows. After looking at the little round tables of displays throughout the room, and the glass shelves that ran along the walls, he still wasn't quite sure what the shop sold.

There were two round racks of clothes in one corner, consisting mostly of colorful veiled skirts and form-fitting tops, the kind Faye liked to wear. But other than that, and a window display of jewelry that appeared to be home-made, most everything else seemed to be jars and glass bottles with silver or gold stoppers, or polished round stones and little velvet bags with gold drawstrings decorating nearly every available surface.

He studied the jewelry in the window then wound his way among the tables, touching the stones, turning them over. He picked up a tiny red velvet bag and tugged the drawstring open, expecting to see powder like Faye had used on CeeCee yesterday. Instead, inside was a vial of amber-colored liquid. He wiggled the little gold stopper open and sniffed. It had a subtle, flowery scent.

"Be careful with that, unless attracting other men is your goal," Faye said as she joined him.

He wrinkled his nose and put the stopper back on the vial.

She laughed and returned it to the red pouch.

"You're saying this is a love potion?" he asked.

"Not love, exactly. More like an aphrodisiac.

It attracts men. I can make you a good deal on one of these, if that's what you're interested in."

He raised a brow. "I think I've already proved where my interests lie." He stepped away from the table, way the hell away from the red pouch.

She laughed again and set the bag on the table. She picked up a gold one instead and tossed it to him. "Here. On the house."

"What is it?"

"It does the same thing as the red one, except that it attracts women. Just in case you want to spice things up in that department."

He dropped the pouch on the nearest table. "Thanks, but no thanks. I don't need any help."

She paused by another table and smoothed her hands over a blue velvet bag. She sashayed seductively to him and slid it into the front pocket of his jeans. "Trust me on this," she breathed. "You'll thank me later."

He groaned. "You're killing me."

Her green eyes twinkled with delight.

Desperate to reengage his brain and to stop thinking about what Faye might look like naked, he waved his hand to encompass the shop. "Is that what this place is all about? Woo-woo love potions?"

She huffed as if he'd just insulted her. "To the uneducated, my powders, lotions and potions might seem 'woo woo,' as you called it. But there's science behind every one of them." She reached down her shirt and pulled out three small pouches hanging from the chain around her neck. "This red one, as you know, is a snake repellant. A very effective one. The gold one is a combination of an antibiotic and a blood coagulant, a clotting agent. If you have a deep cut and can't get to a hospital right away, it might save your life." She dropped the pouches back beneath her shirt.

"What's the purple one for?"

She shook her head and stepped to the door. "You said you wanted to ask the townspeople if they've seen Calvin. Now's your chance. Let's go."

As JAKE WALKED down the wooden boardwalk along the main street with Faye, he couldn't help thinking Mystic Glades would have made the perfect old town in a spaghetti Western movie. Well, minus the oak trees and occasional palms that seemed to fill every space of green between the shops and homes. But the buildings were all wood, like an Old West town, with a wooden sidewalk instead of a paved one. And the stores bore fanciful names such as Callahan's Watering Hole directly across the street from Faye's shop, and Stuffed to the Gills. Jake had expected that one to be a seafood restaurant. But Faye told him it was a taxidermy business. Beside it were Bubba's Take or Trade—a general store of sorts—and Gators and Taters, the only restaurant in town.

"Where is everyone?" he asked. They hadn't passed a single soul since leaving her shop. And there hadn't been any customers in her store the entire time he'd been there.

"Most are at work, in Naples or other places. As you can tell there's not a lot of opportunity to earn a living right here. The few shops we have, like mine, are popular mostly on weekends."

"If everyone's at work right now, then where are we going?"

"SBO, where the few people in town at this time of morning hang out."

Feeling completely out of his element, he followed her as she crossed the dirt road to the other side. "SBO?"

She pointed to the gold lettering on the dark-tinted floor-to-ceiling window that formed the front wall of the building in front of them and went inside.

"Swamp Buggy Outfitters." Jake read the words on the glass. "What the hell is a swamp buggy?" He shook his head and hurried in after her.

The answer to that question met him as soon as he stepped inside. A dune buggy on steroids rested on top of a man-made mountain of rock ten feet from the door. The tires were enormous and just about as tall as Jake. The body of the buggy was a collection of steel pipes with a flat steel platform resting on top. The engine was secured beneath the platform between the two front tires. Metal steps would assist the passengers to the bench seats on top of the platform, just behind the driver's seat. A dark green vinyl tarp attached to metal roll bars shaded the seats. And every inch of the monster was painted in brown-and-green camouflage. Jake had never seen anything like it.

"It can be yours for thirty-six five."

Jake turned around and had to look up to meet the eyes of the man speaking to him. He had a reddish-brown beard at least a foot long and a bushy mustache that curled at the ends. The top of his head was bald.

"You in the market for a buggy?" the man said.

"What exactly would someone do with it?"

He laughed. "Faye did say you weren't from around here." He waved up at the buggy. "That's about the only way to get through some of the more marshy areas of the Everglades, without worrying about stepping on a gator.

You're too high to worry about much of anything up on that platform. Of course if it gets too swampy you have to switch to a canoe or kayak, or even an airboat. Got plenty of canoes and kayaks if you're interested. Only got one airboat and that's mine. Got an ATV, too, but again, that's mine. Of course, everyone borrows it around here from time to time, so it more or less belongs to the town."

Jake looked past the buggy to the canoes hanging on the back wall. Some were suspended from the ceiling. The shop wasn't all that large, but every inch was crammed full of just about everything you'd need outdoors, including tents, sleeping bags and one entire wall of fishing poles. "I'm surprised you don't have hunting rifles in here, too."

"I would but there wouldn't be any point. Too much competition."

"Competition?"

"Locked and Loaded, the gun store at the end of the street."

"Ah." Jake hadn't seen that store, but he hadn't traveled the entire length of the street, either. He held out his hand. "I'm Jake Young, as you already know. I'm a...friend of Faye's." He looked past the man to where Faye stood near a tent display, speaking to a group of about ten men sitting on folding chairs. All of them were nearing sixty years of age, or more.

The man shook his hand in a tight grip that made Jake want to wince.

"Buddy Johnson. And from what I hear, you and Faye are a bit more than friends." He winked and slapped Jake on the back.

He coughed and stumbled forward a few feet.

Buddy laughed and waved for him to follow him over to the others. "Come on. Faye sent me to get you."

Jake suffered through the round of introductions. He'd never met so many Bubbas and Joes in one place before. There was no chance he'd keep them straight. When the introductions were done, he put his arm around Faye's shoulders and tucked her against his side. She put her arm around his waist, much to the delight of some of the men who grinned and whispered to each other.

Faye waved toward two of them. "Joe and Bubba said they may have seen the man you're looking for, honey. Bubba, tell Jake what you told me."

Heat flashed through him at her easy use of the endearment and the way her fingers absently stroked his side. This woman was dangerous in so many ways.

The man she'd called Bubba scratched the white stubble on his jaw before replying. "Two days ago, I was out near Croc Landing when I saw a guy back in the trees and palmettos. Medium build, short brown hair, about five-eight or nine. I remember him because he had a backpack but no gun that I could see. I figured he was an idiot tourist with no common sense and a lousy sense of direction. I was going to see if he needed help finding his way back to wherever he came from, but as soon as he saw me he ducked behind a tree." He shrugged. "Obviously he didn't want my help."

"Where's Croc Landing?" Jake asked.

"Southwest of here, about six miles," Faye said. "Joe, you saw the same man just yesterday, right?"

"Yep. The clothing matched what Bubba said earlier before your Jake came over here—jeans and a dark blue button-up shirt." Joe adjusted the faded orange-and-black Miami Marlins baseball cap on his head. "About four clicks south of where Bubba saw him. Deep in the marsh. I figured the same as Bubba, that the feller was lost. But he took off as soon as he saw me. Definitely didn't want help."

Faye smoothed her hand up Jake's chest. "That has to be Calvin. If someone else were lost out this far there'd have been a story on the news, maybe a missing tourist from an airboat tour. But I haven't heard of anything like that."

He covered her hand with his to maintain his sanity. Her warm fingers were practically burning a hole through his shirt and had him wanting to pull her behind the tent and kiss her senseless.

She winked, obviously enjoying his discomfort. How was he going to keep his hands off her for the rest of this case?

"He didn't seem hurt?" Jake asked.

Both Joe and Bubba shook their heads.

"He has supplies in that backpack," Faye said. "He's obviously lost but doesn't trust any strangers to help him. He must be using a compass. That would explain why he keeps going south instead of north back to the highway."

The men around her all nodded as if what she'd said made perfect sense.

Jake was still wondering about her statement, that Gillette "has" supplies, instead of "*probably* has" supplies. How would she know he had supplies?

"I don't understand," he said. "A compass would make him get more lost?"

"Compasses go crazy around here," she explained. "Just like a lot of electronic equipment, GPS trackers, cell phones. There's something about the swamp in this area that makes things like compasses unreliable. In order to find your way around, you have to rely on landmarks and the sun or stars."

"Do you mind if I ask why anyone would actually choose to live in a place like this, in the middle of nowhere?"

The friendly looks on the men's faces faded. Faye gave him an aggravated look.

"What?" he asked.

She grabbed his hand. "Come on. Let's get out of here before Buddy decides to use you as target practice for his fancy new crossbow."

They'd just reached the street when the Buddy in question leaned out the door. "Faye, hold up. You going out past Croc Landing to look for that fellow right now?"

"We're leaving as soon as I grab my gear from the shop."

"Hang on a sec." He disappeared back inside. A couple of minutes later he hurried back out holding two dark green backpacks. One of them was noticeably larger than the other. Buddy heaved it at Jake, who staggered back when he caught it against his chest.

"This thing weighs a ton," Jake said.

Buddy arched a brow. "I might have accidentally distributed the weight more in that pack than Faye's. My bad." The sour look he gave Jake told him it wasn't an accident. He handed the much lighter-looking, smaller pack to Faye. "Those packs have everything you need in case you get caught out past sundown. I'd consider it a favor if you take them. You can let me know how the new gear holds up. There's a tent in the pack your man's holding. Do you need any weapons?"

"Of course not. I'm packing." She slid her arms through the straps of the backpack and buckled the strap that tightened it against her waist. She stood on tiptoe and kissed his cheek. "Thanks, Buddy. You're a sweetheart."

He flushed and stepped back. "Be careful, darlin'."

"Always."

Jake rolled his eyes and hoisted the heavy pack onto his shoulders, fastening the straps the way Faye had done. If his pack weighed less than sixty pounds, it wasn't by much.

Faye waved goodbye to Buddy and grabbed Jake's hand. "Come on." She started down the street, away from the shop.

"My car's back that way," he said. "From what your friends told us, Gillette was at least eight miles away yesterday. He could be a lot more than that by now."

"Cars can't reach Croc Landing. It's all marsh."

"We're going to hike the whole way?"

She gave him an exasperated look. "Do you always complain this much?"

He clamped his mouth shut and pulled her to the boardwalk as a car went by, the first he'd seen since he'd been there. They continued toward the end of the street, passing several more shops. When he saw the church at the very end, he couldn't help but laugh.

Faye shot him a death glare.

He coughed and forced the amusement off his face until she turned around and started walking again. He would have loved to snap a picture of the sign above the church, but he figured Faye would probably drop him on his ass again if he did. So, instead, he made a mental note to tell Dex about it the next time they spoke. His business partner would get a real kick out of a church called Last Chance advertising "over five hundred saved" just like a fast-food restaurant advertising how many burgers it had sold.

The street dead-ended behind the church, but Faye didn't even slow down. She headed into the trees, with Jake hurrying to catch up. Fifty yards in, the solid ground ended and the marsh began.

Faye stopped and faced him. "Take off the pack."

He didn't question her dictate. This was her

domain and he was more than willing to take the heavy pack off. He unclipped the strap at his waist and slipped out of the shoulder straps. The pack dropped to the ground with a solid thunk.

She crouched down and opened it.

Jake swore when he saw what was inside on top. Rocks. Big, heavy rocks like the ones used to build the fake mountain where Buddy's swamp buggy was perched back at SBO. He counted ten rocks before Faye finished taking them out and then handed the pack back to him.

The weight had easily been cut in half. He slung it onto his shoulders and fastened the straps.

"How did you know?" he asked.

"By how heavy it seemed when Buddy threw it to you. I figured he was teaching you a lesson in manners. Lesson learned?"

He let out a deep breath. "Lesson learned."

"Good. Let's go. It'll take most of the day to navigate to Croc Landing. It's in the most treacherous part of the swamp and hard to reach. If we don't find Calvin there, I want to get a good distance from the Landing to a higher, safer spot before dark."

He looked out over the marsh, wondering how deep it was and whether there were any alligators hiding in the mud. "Can't we borrow Buddy's swamp buggy and make it there faster? And safer?" He'd much rather be higher up where nothing could bite him.

"That swamp buggy costs more than I'd make in two years running my shop. I'm not about to ask him to loan it to me. And I'd have to go the back way, around the main waterways, to get there. I've never been that way on my own."

Jake sighed with disappointment. "Okay. Then how do we get to Croc Landing? On foot?"

She headed past him and bent down beside a pile of leaves. After fumbling with what appeared to be a plastic buckle, she swept the leaves back, which turned out to be part of a camouflaged tarp.

Jake groaned when he saw what was underneath.

Faye gave him a smug look. "Come on, city slicker. I'm going to teach you how to navigate a swamp in a canoe."

## Chapter Seven

The canoe slid quietly through a cluster of lily pads, their yellow flowers perfuming the air with each dip of Jake's oar into the water. The knobby knees of cypress tree roots stuck up out of the swamp beneath the canopy of branches over the shallows. Faye loved the swamp, with its musty smells and constant chorus of singing birds and frogs, and the occasional bellow of an alligator. She would often spend an entire weekend out in the bog, with just her canoe for company, taking in the sights, enjoying the freedom. But this time, she wasn't alone. And she was finding, to her surprise, that sharing the majestic world of the Everglades with Jake was even more fun than usual.

When she pointed out birds or plants, naming them, explaining about their habitats and how they fit into the ecosystem, he listened intently, asking questions and seeming to enjoy the marsh as much as she did as his understanding of it grew. She hadn't expected that from a man who'd spent most of his life in the city or walking the beach. He'd surprised her in other ways, too, such as how well he was doing with the canoe.

She'd been half teasing when she'd said she'd teach him. She'd assumed he'd been canoeing at least a handful of times in his life, just maybe not in a swamp. She'd been shocked to find that he'd never even been in a canoe.

In spite of that shameful admission, he'd been a quick learner. Faye had planned on paddling at first to show him how. But Jake had been horrified by that idea. He wasn't about to sit and do nothing while a woman did the work. His old-fashioned ideas were silly to Faye, but she also thought it was sweet. And she thought it would be fun to play along and see how many times he'd get them stuck on a submerged tree or mired in mud before he admitted he needed her help. Surprisingly, he hadn't gotten stuck even once. He followed her instructions to the letter, and was soon paddling them down the waterway like a pro.

She would have liked to sit there facing him, admiring the way his muscles bunched in his arms with each powerful stroke of the paddle, but she had to navigate. Which meant facing away from him, calling out orders to turn, slow down or speed up.

Croc Landing turned out to be a disappointment for Jake, who'd expected to see dozens of the reptiles sunbathing on the banks of the waterway. Instead, the bank was deserted, which suited Faye just fine.

"I thought you were afraid of alligators," she said.

"Let's go with respectful. Wary. But as long as we're inside the canoe, we're safe. So I thought it would be cool to see a bunch of them on the bank."

"Since we have to step out on that bank, I'm happy there aren't any around right now."

He looked at the water with renewed vigilance. "Good point. If it's called Croc Landing, why are we talking alligators? Aren't there any crocodiles around here?"

"We get a few crocodiles but they thrive more in the saltwater marshes. Mostly we have alligators."

"Then why is this place called Croc Landing?"

"Because 'Croc Landing' sounds better on a tourist pamphlet than 'Gator Landing.'"

"Ah, the almighty dollar at work. I didn't see any tourist fliers in Mystic Glades. Does Buddy take people out on his airboat?"

She laughed. "I'm pretty sure he'd be insulted if you asked him that. He doesn't like the idea of tourists traipsing through our precious 'Glades. It's the airboat tour companies a bit farther south that sometimes bring people up as far as Croc Landing. No one in Mystic Glades would dream of welcoming people from the outside."

"Your friends at SBO seemed pretty nice to me. And Freddie and Amy were nice, too, even though I'm an outsider."

"Yeah, but we lied and told them you were with me. Makes a big difference." She pointed to the right where she wanted to land the canoe.

Jake speared the water with the oar and guided them toward shore. "You didn't grow up in Mystic Glades, right? But they accept you as one of their own. That's because of your friend, Amber Callahan?"

She nodded, some of her fun with the canoe trip evaporating. "Yes."

"I don't remember meeting her. Does she help Freddie in the bar?"

She half turned, looking back at him. "Amber and I lost touch with each other a few years ago. She stopped returning my letters. When I...needed to move to a new place, I came to Mystic Glades, hoping to reestablish our friendship. But when I got here I found out she'd gotten lost and died out in the swamp. That's why my mail went unanswered."

Jake winced. "Sorry. I didn't mean to bring up unhappy memories."

She nodded, and forced thoughts of Amber away. "Over here." She pointed to a place that seemed to offer the easiest access to the "beach," such as it was.

The bottom of the canoe ground against the shallows until the nose wedged into the sand. Faye reassured herself there weren't any reptiles waiting to pounce on her from the water before jumping out of the canoe. She held it steady while Jake moved to the prow. He hopped out and together they pulled the canoe up the incline about twenty feet from the water's edge. They stowed it beneath an oak tree and covered it with the tarp.

Faye pointed out some landmarks—twisted trees and groups of rocks—that they could use to find the canoe on their way back, rather than rely on the GPS on Jake's fancy cell phone.

Two hours later, after hiking through the area around the Landing in concentric circles and finding nothing, Faye called an end to the search.

"I think it's safe to say he's not here. We'll make camp for the night and head out to where

Joe thinks he saw Calvin in the morning. It's a bit of a hike."

By the time they reached a good camping spot, the sun was sinking low on the horizon. But Faye was pleased with their progress. They had a good, relatively safe area to set up camp for the night and could resume their search for Calvin in the morning. On foot and with only a limited knowledge of the area from the few times he'd been to Mystic Glades, Calvin wouldn't make nearly as good time as Faye and Jake. She was confident they'd find him before the next day was out.

As with the canoeing instructions earlier, Jake was a quick learner at how to set up camp. Soon they had the small dome-tent up and some netting erected between the trees near the tent to dissuade small animals on foot. Little bells on the netting would alert them if something got caught in the net, or if something bigger was on the prowl.

Jake surveyed their temporary home. "What about alligators? Will the nets stop them?"

"Doubtful, but we're pretty far from the water. We should be fine here."

He didn't look as if he believed her. He patted the pistol holstered on his waist. "Hopefully I won't have to use this."

She pulled up her pant legs to reveal her

knife strapped on the outside of one boot and her pistol strapped on the outside of the other. "I've got us covered."

He gave her a lopsided grin and shook his head. "I wondered where you were hiding those when you told Buddy you were packing."

"A girl's got to protect herself."

He glanced up at the tree limbs hanging over their campsite. "What about snakes?"

She flicked the silver chain around her neck. "Snake repellant. I grabbed a new bag before I left the shop."

"That's fine for an emergency, but I'd rather not get close enough to a snake to use that."

She laughed. "Don't worry. If you get attacked I promise I'll help you fend off the snake."

"What if you're the one who gets attacked?"

"I'll just have to trust you to save me."

He nodded, his expression serious. "I won't let anything happen to you."

She slid her hand up his chest. "See that you don't."

He took a quick step back, forcing her to drop her hand. "Since I don't see a bathroom or a porta-pottie around here, I'm going to take a walk."

Disappointment shot through her. She'd felt freed last night, at peace with her belief that he had a good soul, that she could trust him. She'd decided to pursue the incredible chemistry between them and just enjoy being with him for however long they had together. But every time she tried to initiate anything more than a casual touch, he pulled away. It had practically taken her attacking him back at the store to get him to kiss her.

But, oh my, did he know how to kiss once he'd let himself go.

She sighed at the memory and pointed to a break in the trees to the west. "You go that way and I'll go this way." She grabbed a latrine kit from the pack and tossed it to him. "You're a smart guy. I'm sure you can figure out how to use that."

JAKE DIDN'T STOP until he was a good fifty yards from their campsite. He found a clearing on a slight rise and checked the bars on his phone. Only two—hopefully that would be enough. He took another minute to scout the nearby bushes and trees looking for snakes and alligators, but he seemed to be alone. Then again, a hungry reptile could be hiding in the dirt nearby and he might never see it. Just to be safe, he pulled out his pistol and set it on a fallen tree log beside him as he sat with his phone.

He absently studied the latrine kit while he dialed Dex Lassiter's number. The green vinyl bag contained a small hand shovel, an equally small roll of toilet paper and antibacterial hand wipes. He laughed and set it aside.

"Lassiter," the voice on the phone answered.

"Dex, it's Jake."

"Well, it's about damn time. I was seriously considering reporting *you* as a missing person. I haven't heard from you since you found Gillette's car."

"I know, I know. I've been busy." He quickly summarized what had happened since then. "Faye thinks we'll find Calvin sometime tomorrow. I don't have a lot of phone time, so you'll have to relay the information to Quinn for me."

"No problem. Is Faye armed?"

"When is she not? She's got a gun and knife strapped to her boots."

"We should call Holder. Get some backup."

"Quinn gave strict instructions to keep this on the down low. And if Holder makes the catch—"

"We don't get paid. Yeah, I know. Still. I'm not sure the danger is worth it."

Jake tapped the log beside him. "Faye has a good heart. She loves animals and plants, and risks her life to help people. Yesterday she saved a man from a boa constrictor. She's not dangerous to anyone."

"Tell that to Genovese."

Jake tightened his hand around the phone. "Yeah, about that. How much do we really know about the case other than what Quinn told us?"

Dex groaned.

"What?" Jake demanded.

"You're falling for her."

"Shut up. I am not. I'm just curious. The woman I've met doesn't mesh with what we've been told. I'd like to see some details from the case. Just get the file and double-check that no red flags go up, all right?"

A bush rustled behind him. He jerked around. Was that a shadow? A deeper black than the rest of the darkness as the sun slid lower in the sky? He grabbed his pistol and stood. "Faye? Is that you?"

"Jake, you okay?" Dex asked.

He waited but didn't hear anything else. The shadow no longer seemed to be there. Were his eyes playing tricks on him?

"Jake?"

"I'm still here. Thought I saw something. You're going to look into the case, right?"

Dex groaned again. "Okay, okay. I think it's a complete waste of time. But since you're the one out there putting your life on the line, the least I can do is get Quinn to email me a copy of the case file."

"Sounds good. I'll try to call you tomorrow but I don't know when I'll be able to get away or have cell coverage. Don't freak if you don't hear from me right away."

He ended the call and answered nature's call before starting back to camp. That dark shadow he'd seen, or thought he saw, had the hairs standing up on the back of his neck. He stopped a few times to listen and peer into the underbrush. But he never figured out what had caused that shadow. Unless it was his overactive imagination.

When he reached the campsite and stepped over the netting, Faye was kneeling by a small fire, stirring a pot on top of a metal rack. Her long hair was twisted into a thick braid hanging down her back.

She looked up in question as he sat beside her. "You were gone awhile. I was about to come looking for you."

"I took a short walk, looked around."

Her brows rose. "You find what you were looking for?"

He was careful to keep his expression blank so he wouldn't give anything away. "I didn't see any tracks from Gillette, but I did get the feeling I was being watched. Thought I heard some bushes move as if something big had passed behind them. Are there any bears around here?"

She smiled and turned her attention to stirring the mouthwatering soup or stew that was in the pot. "We've got some black bears here and there, but they're typically too afraid to go near people. There are some foxes out here, too, raccoons, even an occasional bobcat. But those are rare."

He bent forward to get a better smell of the food. "Would a bobcat trigger the bells and netting we've got strung up?"

She pushed him back. "Patience. It's almost done. And no, probably not. A bobcat would just jump out of a tree on top of us."

He looked up at the branches hanging over them.

Faye laughed. "For such a large man, you sure are skittish."

"I'd just prefer not to become a meal for some predator while I'm out here. That's not the way I want to go out."

"Get the bowls and spoons, will you?" She pointed to a small cloth lying in the dirt with the dishes sitting on it next to some bottles of water.

He handed her the bowls one at a time as

she ladled out the meal. While they sat down to eat, he handed her one of the water bottles. She nodded her thanks.

"This smells incredible." He took a large spoonful of the stew, which was full of potatoes, carrots and chunks of meat. "Wow, that's amazing. Best beef stew I think I've ever had. What's the brand?"

"Brand? You think this came from a can?"

He paused with the next spoonful halfway to his mouth and eyed it suspiciously. "It didn't?"

She shook her head. "Nope."

He put the spoon back in his bowl, untouched. "Did you catch, skin and cook a rabbit while I was gone?"

She laughed. "No. Buddy gave us some stew his wife made. It's Grade A, Uncle Sam-inspected, one hundred percent pure beef. Relax."

He grinned and quickly emptied his bowl, and a second one after that. Faye showed him how to clean the dishes without water and tightly store them and the empty plasticware that the stew had come in so that animals wouldn't smell it and be attracted to the food.

After turning on a small battery-operated lantern, Faye put the fire out. Jake had wanted to keep it lit to scare critters away. But Faye had insisted on dousing the flames to ensure they didn't accidentally start a marsh fire. He reluctantly agreed and helped her stow everything back in their packs, all ready for the morning. The only thing left was to go to bed.

The tiny tent would barely sleep one, let alone two. Jake didn't think he'd be able to get any sleep with Faye lying that close to him. And even if he did, he was worried he might be drawn to her in his sleep and do something he'd regret. Well, *regret* might be too strong a word. He'd love nothing more than to finish what he and Faye had started in the back room of her store earlier today. But it wasn't right, not when almost everything that came out of his mouth was a lie.

"We should probably take turns on watch," he said, "just in case some animal wanders too close."

She picked up the lantern and took his hand in hers. "That's what the nets and bells are for. Plus we'll zip up the tent. Don't worry. I'll protect you." She tugged him toward the tent.

"I'm the one who'll protect you," he grumbled but didn't argue anymore.

Even with the vents in the tent, it was too warm to get inside the sleeping bags. Jake lay on top of his. He kept his clothes on, both out of respect for Faye and to add an extra layer of protection between them if he reached for her in his sleep.

Faye had no such concerns. After taking off her boots and setting her knife and gun at the foot of the tent, she shimmied out of her tight jeans, leaving her in her lacy green top and—oh, God—matching lacy green thong. With a tiny lime-green bow.

His mouth watered at the thought of that delicate, little bow, of grasping it with his teeth and tugging it down, down, down. Realizing where he was staring, he forced his gaze up to meet hers. She smiled, a slow, lazy smile that promised things that made him almost whimper out loud.

*No, she's off-limits. She doesn't know you're working for the FBI. It's not right to make love to her with so many lies between us, especially since there's no way we could ever be together once the truth comes out.*

He shuddered and rolled over, scooting as far away from her tantalizing heat as possible. "Good night," he rasped through his tight throat as he clutched his pillow to keep from reaching for her.

A deep sigh met his statement. "Good night." The lantern went out, plunging the tent into darkness.

FAYE ROLLED ONTO her back and stared up at the complete blackness of the tent roof above her. The base of the dome-shaped tent was about seven feet long and four feet wide, and yet so far Jake had managed to keep his long, thickly muscled body from touching her in any way. Frustration was making her curl her nails into her palms.

She knew he wanted her. Just as he knew she wanted him. So what was the problem? Was he sleeping? She didn't think so. His breathing wasn't the deep and even breathing of someone off in dreamland. If anything, his breathing was too carefully controlled, as if he was trying not to think about her lying beside him.

Not sleeping together, or rather only *sleeping* together and doing nothing else, was probably the wisest choice. He didn't know about her past, that it was like a ticking time bomb waiting to explode if the Tuscaloosa police figured out where she was. And she didn't really know anything about him other than he was a police officer trying his hand at being a private investigator, trying to find the one person who could blow her world apart.

No, making love to the incredibly attractive, delicious-looking Jake Young made no sense whatsoever. But since when did chemistry between a man and a woman ever make sense? Right now, at this moment, all that mattered was that she was on fire for him. And she knew he was on fire for her. If everything went to hell in the morning, so be it. But, tonight, for the first time in thirteen months, she just wanted to feel, to enjoy having a man desire her and hold her in his arms. For once, she wanted to let her worries and fears melt away and live in the moment. She wanted this, *needed* this. And thanks to the condoms she'd discovered that Buddy had included in her backpack—she was completely prepared.

She sat up and made quick work of her braid, finger-combing her tresses until they hung past her hips to the tent floor. She remembered the way Jake had plunged his fingers into her hair this morning when he'd kissed her. He liked her hair, and she would ruthlessly take advantage of that.

Next she shimmied out of her thong. Just the whisper of the material against her as she pulled it off was almost too much for her nerve endings to take. The way Jake had stared at the bow on her panties had made her clench with need and anticipation. That same need rose up in her now as she pulled her shirt over her head and tossed it to the foot of the tent. Her necklace followed. Lastly she unhooked her bra and added it to the pile of discarded clothes.

Shoot, the condoms. Where were they? In her jeans. In her wishful thinking earlier when he'd left camp for his "walk" she'd slid three of the foil packets in her pocket. She scrambled to the end of the tent to find where she'd put her jeans.

"Faye? Is something wrong?" Jake called out.

She found the foil packets and clutched them in her hands. "Not anymore. Or at least, not for long."

"What? Did you hear something outside the tent?"

She could hear him moving behind her. She turned around just as the lantern light clicked on.

He was sitting up, the light in his hand. His jaw dropped open, his eyes widened, and he went still as a statue.

Faye looked down at the shiny foil packets clutched in her right hand. There was no way he couldn't see them, or not know what they were. She was completely naked, her breasts jutting out, her hair hanging down around her hips. What did someone say in a situation like this?

She cleared her throat and smiled. "Um, surprise?"

# Chapter Eight

Faye stared at Jake, just three feet away, waiting. His eyes swept down her body, lingering on her breasts, the apex between her thighs. But he didn't move. She wasn't even sure he was breathing.

"Jake. *Say* something."

"Can't," he choked.

"Then *do* something. I'm starting to feel a little silly here."

His eyes finally rose. "You're absolutely exquisite," he whispered, his voice ragged, raw.

Her belly tightened at his words. "I'm still feeling silly since I'm the only one here without any clothes. I'd appreciate it if you'd take your clothes off. I've got something else for you to wear."

He frowned. "What do you want me to wear?"

She held up one of the condom packets.

He visibly shuddered. But he still didn't move to take her.

"Jake?"

"You don't know me," he whispered, for some reason looking completely miserable.

"I know what I need to know," she said. "You're strong, smart, protective even when you don't need to be. You're a great listener even though I probably bored you to death on the canoe trip."

He shook his head. "You weren't boring."

"I want you, Jake. Don't make me beg."

"I'm going to hell for this."

"Take me with you."

He reached for her and lifted her onto his lap, straddling him. He sank his fingers into her hair and shook his head in wonder. "I've never seen a more beautiful woman."

She sank against him, her breasts flattening against his chest as she wrapped her arms behind his neck. "You say the sweetest things."

He crushed her to him, devouring her in an openmouthed frenzy as if he was dying and she was his only hope of salvation. Their kiss this morning had been mild compared with the heat they generated now. His lips moved against hers, stoking her desire higher and higher, making her moan deep in her throat. She could kiss him forever and never get enough. He was like a master craftsman plying his trade, wrenching every ounce of pleasure her body was capable of feeling, and then bringing her up another level until she thought she'd go out of her mind for wanting him. Her entire body pulsed with need, an ache of longing so deep she thought she'd die if he didn't make love to her right then.

She wrenched her lips from his and reached down between them, desperate to feel him. She whimpered at the feel of him through his clothes. "Take. These. Off," she demanded.

He swallowed, hard, and gently set her down on the sleeping bag. He unbuttoned his jeans but he was moving much too slowly. She shoved him down onto his back and went to work on his zipper, then yanked his pants down his legs, shucking them off and tossing them behind her.

He laughed, then sucked in a deep breath when she shoved her hands beneath his boxers. She stroked his velvety soft skin, reveling in his hardness. She bent down and kissed him, tasted him.

A guttural curse escaped his clenched teeth. He grabbed her and pulled her up his body and captured her lips with his. When he finally broke the kiss they were both struggling to catch their breath. He yanked off his shirt and went to work on the Velcro straps of his bullet-resistant vest.

Faye blinked in surprise. "Why are you wearing that?"

He looked at his vest, as if surprised himself, and shrugged. "Habit. I always wear it when I'm working a case." He quickly discarded the rest of his clothes then pulled her against him, skin against skin, softness against hardness as he worshipped every inch of her body with his mouth.

She was about to beg for mercy when he finally settled himself on top of her at her entrance.

"Wait, wait," she cried out.

He shuddered and stilled against her. "Please don't say you changed your mind," he begged.

"What? No, no. Hell, no." She giggled and grabbed one of the foil packets. After rolling the condom onto him, she gave him one long, exquisite stroke. "Now," she said. "Now, Jake."

But he didn't take her. Instead, he kissed her again as his hands slid all over her body, stroking, kneading, feathering across her skin until she thought she would die from the pleasure of it. Every nerve ending in her body seemed to be at a fever pitch, ready to explode.

She tore her mouth from his and reached down between them to position him again. "If you don't do it now," she whispered against his lips, "I'm going to shoot you."

He laughed and surged forward, thrusting inside her. She threw her head back in ecstasy at the feel of him stretching and filling her. She scored her nails down his back and lightly bit his shoulder as he plunged into her, harder and faster. She matched his rhythm, wrapping her legs around him and trying to pull him in deeper.

Every movement of him inside her, every stroke of his hands against her between their bodies, every touch of his lips against her skin sent her higher, and higher until she didn't think she could possibly go higher. And then he took her there, up, up, up, whispering in her ear, telling her how he loved her body and what else he wanted to do with her as he shuddered and plunged into her over and over again.

Her climax washed over her in an explosion of feeling that had her screaming his name and sinking her nails into his shoulders. He rode her through her climax, drawing it out, sending her up and over the edge even as the last waves of her first climax were still rippling through her. She screamed again. He tightened inside her and this time he followed her, clasping her against his body as wave after wave of ecstasy crashed through both of them. They collapsed back against the sleeping bags in an exhausted but thoroughly sated, boneless tangle of arms and legs.

Faye lay there, her breaths rattling out of her as her heart struggled to stop racing and calm down to a natural rhythm again. Sweat slicked her skin and beaded between her breasts, slowly running down her belly. Behind her, Jake's labored breaths came quick and fast like hers and she could feel his heart pounding against her back.

"Wow," she finally managed. "I've never, ever…"

"Me, neither." His voice was husky and deeper than usual, sending a delightful shiver straight to her core.

He wrapped his arm around her waist and pulled her tighter against him, spooning his body to hers. She loved the feel of his lightly furred chest against her back. In fact, she loved everything about him. Plus, he was a Sagittarius and she was a Libra. Had fate brought them together? She automatically reached for the purple velvet pouch on her necklace before remembering she'd taken it off.

His fingers lightly stroked her belly, warming her all over, making her feel cherished, and for the first time in her life…*loved*. Loved? She stiffened at that ridiculous thought. No one could care about someone that deeply when they were practically strangers.

His arm tightened. "What's wrong?"

"I just…we don't even know each other, and here we are…"

His deep sigh sounded near her ear. "I know. You're right. I shouldn't have—"

"Oh yes, you should have. No take backs. No regrets. That's not what I'm saying."

"Then what *are* you saying?"

"I want to know more about you. I'd like to know more about the man who just blew my mind."

He laughed, his hot breath washing against her neck. He trailed his fingertips up to that same, sensitive spot and stroked her skin, making her shiver. He pressed a quick kiss to her there.

"What is it that you want to know?"

"Where are you from? Do you have a family?" She sucked in a breath. "Do you have a girlfriend?"

He scooted back and gently rolled her over so she was flat on her back looking up at him. His eyes were dark, his expression intent.

"If I was in a relationship with someone, what we just did wouldn't have happened." He gently smoothed her hair back from her face. "I grew up in North Florida, in Saint Augustine. I don't have any family, not anymore."

She slid her hands up his chest, delighting in the way his muscles flexed beneath her hands and the way the crisp hairs tickled her fingers. "Not anymore?"

"My parents died a long time ago. It was just me and my sister for years. But she's… gone now."

His voice was flat, as if he was trying to mask his pain, but she saw it in the tension around his eyes, and the lines of concentration on his brow. She cupped his face and brought him down closer so she could kiss the worry lines away.

"I'm sorry for your loss," she whispered. "What happened?"

He rolled onto his back. She figured she'd asked him too sensitive, too personal a question. But then he reached for her and tucked her against his side, her breasts snugged up against his ribs. She sighed with contentment and rested her hand on his chest.

"She married my best friend," he said, his voice barely above a whisper. "A couple of years later, there was a home invasion. She was killed."

"Oh my gosh, I'm so, so sorry. What happened to her husband?"

"Rafe? He survived. He was knocked out, shot, but he made it. Shelby didn't."

She traced the lines of his stomach muscles. "You blame him. Why?"

He shook his head. "No. I don't blame him. I did, for a long time. I let hate and resentment build up inside me to the point that I made some very bad decisions. It almost cost both of us our lives. And it took a very special person, his new wife—Darby—to eventually bring us back together. But even though he forgave me, I couldn't forgive myself. I needed a fresh start. So when an old college friend contacted me about starting a private investigation firm with him, I took leave from my police job to jump at the chance, see if it was worth giving up my law enforcement career for good. So here I am. What about you? Did you come from a large family?"

She stiffened, her hand going still on his stomach.

He put his fingers beneath her chin and turned her head to look at him. "I'm not asking as an investigator, Faye. I'm asking as the man who just made love to you, the man who genuinely wants to know more about the extraordinary woman that you are. If it makes you uncomfortable talking about family, tell me something else. But don't shut down. Don't push me away."

She doubted there was any way for him to truly separate himself from his job, but the intimacy between them created by him sharing about his past had her wanting to share with him, as well. She carefully waded through the pieces of her life in her mind, picking out what she could share without giving up the secrets that could destroy her.

"I never had a family, not a real one. My parents died when I was too young to remember them. I was put in foster care, starting in Mobile. I was shuffled from family to family, place to place."

"You were never adopted?"

"No. I've always been a bit…headstrong, and odd I suppose, compared to most people. I didn't fit in with the picture of the perfect daughter that families were looking for."

He hugged her close and pressed a kiss on her forehead before lying flat again. "I'm sorry, Faye. That had to be so hard."

"Early on it was, but in my later years, at the last foster home, I met…another girl, close to my age. We both loved animals and plants and exploring. We wanted to save the environment and educate people about the precious habitats around them. We became each other's confidantes, like real sisters."

"What was her name?"

"Doesn't matter."

He gave her a brief hug. "Okay. What happened to her? Is she okay? Do you still see each other?"

"After college, we went to work together, contracting out for major landscaping jobs. I used my education in plants and ecology to design the most amazing gardens. And she used her architecture background to add the hardscape. And yes, we do occasionally see each other, though not as often as I'd like."

After a few moments of silence, he seemed to understand that she wasn't going to say anything else. She couldn't, not without telling him too much, not without endangering herself. He turned on his side, facing her. His mouth dipped down to her shoulder. He lightly sucked, sending heat flashing through her.

He kissed a trail across her collarbone before pulling her in for a deep, mind-numbing kiss that had her melting all over again. When he hardened against her, she broke the kiss, looking down in shock.

"Already? You can't possibly—" she started to say.

"With you, yes, I can," he answered back.

She grinned. "Jake, remember the blue velvet pouch I put in the pocket of your jeans? Trust me when I say that you *really* want to get that." She licked her lips, slowly, deliberately.

He dived for his jeans.

JAKE CAME AWAKE SLOWLY, reluctantly. He didn't want to open his eyes and face the repercussions of last night. Making love to Faye had ranked up there with one of the most incredible experiences of his life. Especially after they'd opened that blue velvet pouch. He shuddered just thinking about it.

But even though making love to her had been practically life altering, it was also one of the dumbest mistakes he could have made. Nothing had changed to make it okay to use her in that way when she had no idea why he was really here. When they found Gillette, she was going to hate him. And he wouldn't blame her one bit.

Perhaps knowing that he could never hold her again was the real reason he lay on the sleeping bag resisting getting up. He could sense the sunlight, knew it was morning and that he needed to get on with the hunt for Gillette. But if he got up he'd have to let go of

Faye. And doing that was harder, much harder, than it should have been.

He ran his hands over her silky hair and slid his fingers in it. Or at least, he tried to. Her hair felt silky, soft, but he couldn't distinguish the individual strands like last night. And her hair was...warm?

Hot breath panted against his face. A sand-papery tongue licked his neck.

Jake's eyes flew open. He stared into a pair of deep green eyes. But they weren't Faye's.

They belonged to a black panther.

He scrambled out of the tent, expecting to feel the panther's claws at any moment, raking down his back and slicing his skin open. He'd just cleared the tent entrance when the panther tackled him from behind, its heavy body knocking Jake to the ground.

He twisted around, aiming a punch at the panther's jaw. But his fist met nothing but air. The panther had jumped off him and bounded across the clearing. Jake scrambled to his knees to see where the animal went. His veins turned to ice when he saw Faye walking toward him from the trees. The panther was headed straight for her.

"Faye, look out!" Jake grabbed one of the small branches from the cold fire pit from last night and ran after the panther.

Faye's eyes widened with alarm.

Oh, God. He wasn't going to reach her in time. "Faye!"

The panther jumped at her. Faye disappeared beneath a black ball of fur as she fell to the ground. Jake reached them and pulled back the branch like a bat, ready to let it fly.

"Don't hurt him!" Faye yelled, rolling with the panther out of Jake's reach.

Jake stopped with the branch up in the air, blinking down in shock. Faye was on her knees, her arms around the panther's neck, glaring at him as if he was the bad guy.

"He's harmless. Leave him alone," she said.

He slowly lowered the branch, his heart slamming so hard he could feel each beat. "Harmless?" he choked. "He's a wild animal. He attacked me in the tent."

She rolled her eyes. "He probably cuddled with you and licked you. He certainly couldn't have attacked you." She pulled his mouth open. "See, no teeth. No claws, either, except on his hind legs. And I don't see any claw marks on you to justify you threatening to hit him." She hugged the panther and stroked it as if it were a large house cat. "There, there, Sampson. It's okay. Don't be scared."

Jake should have felt ridiculous standing there naked while Faye hugged a toothless, clawless panther as if it were a domestic house cat. But all he could think about was the sheer panic and overwhelming fear when he'd thought she was about to be mauled. Everything else had faded away. All that mattered was reaching her in time to save her.

He'd been willing to sacrifice his own body to protect her, instead of taking the extra few seconds to retrieve his gun from inside the tent, which would have been a hell of a lot smarter than grabbing a tree branch. But he hadn't wanted to risk those extra few seconds. He'd fully intended to wrap his arms around the wild cat and give it something else to chomp on if that would keep Faye from getting hurt and give her time to get a gun to protect herself.

"Jake? Jake are you okay?" She shoved the cat away from her and stood. She looked him up and down, as if searching for injuries. "What's wrong?"

He strode over to her and grabbed her shoulders. "What's *wrong*? What's wrong is that I thought you were about to be hurt, or killed. And I was too far away. My God, I couldn't reach you, I couldn't…" He closed his eyes briefly and swallowed. When he opened them again he looked at the panther, lying on its side, calmly licking its fur. "Next time one of

your 'pets' is skulking around, warn me," he
bit out.

He stalked back toward the tent to get dressed.

FAYE'S MOUTH DROPPED open as Jake strode away
from her, his golden skin gleaming and rippling with muscles in the morning sunlight
peeking through the trees overhead. His anger
showed in every step, every jerky movement
of his beautiful body until he disappeared into
the tent.

It hadn't even occurred to her to tell him
about Sampson. The cat often followed her on
her jaunts through the woods. But he usually
stayed closer to the store so he wouldn't miss
a meal. She and Amy fed him ground-up meat
every day out the back door. The cat tended to
be shy around strangers, with good reason. Its
past as an abused circus animal still made it
skittish. She'd never expected him to show up
with Jake here.

And she'd never expected Jake would get so
upset, all because he thought she was going
to get hurt. She couldn't help but smile. Her
instincts about him had been right. He was
a good man. After everything that had gone
wrong in the past few years, finally everything
was starting to go right. When she and Jake

found Calvin, they'd tell him about the brother he never knew he had. And then they could all return to Mystic Glades together.

## Chapter Nine

Getting over his earlier scare about the panther hurting Faye was proving to be more difficult than it should have been. Jake sat silently through their breakfast of beef jerky, granola bars and water. Faye kept giving him questioning looks, but he just couldn't say anything. He still wanted to shake her.

He'd never been so scared in his life. And that scared the hell out of him. He was losing his perspective, getting too attached. He couldn't deny that now. And that made this trip even more dangerous than it had started out to be.

After packing their gear, they headed out, searching in a grid pattern southwest of where they'd made camp. Nearly three hours later, they found what they'd been looking for—footprints. According to Faye, who was a much better tracker than Jake could ever hope to be, the prints were recent, made in the past day. It was unlikely anyone else would be in this area except for Gillette.

They headed through the trees, occasionally trekking across broad swaths of saw grass marshy areas. Jake kept his gun holstered close at hand, expecting to step on an alligator any minute. But Faye seemed to know exactly what she was doing. She knew the signs to look for, and their jaunt was largely uneventful.

As they neared the edge of another "tree island" and were about to step under the shade of a group of pine trees, Jake put his hand on Faye's shoulder. He'd had enough of the tension and uncomfortable silence between them. And it was time he set it to rights.

She turned with a question in her eyes.

He'd meant to apologize, but instead he framed her face in his hands and kissed her. It was a soft, gentle kiss, at first anyway. But it seemed that any time he touched her he couldn't control himself. He groaned low in his throat and deepened the kiss, crushing his lips to hers. And in spite of how surly he'd been all morning since the "panther incident," she responded with just as much enthusiasm as she had last night.

When he realized he was thinking about pulling her down to the filthy ground and making love to her right there, he forced himself to end the kiss and step back.

"Wow," she said. "What was that for?"

"For being an ass, I suppose. I'm sorry about getting so angry with you earlier. I just…when I saw—"

She pressed her finger against his lips. "Don't apologize. You were upset because you thought I was going to get hurt, and because I didn't tell you about Sampson. I understand, and you're right. I should have told you about him." She stood on tiptoe and pulled his head down to hers so she could press a quick, soft kiss against his lips. "Thank you for caring. It's been a long time since anyone did."

That soft admission sent another punch of guilt straight to his gut. "How did you end up with a pet panther?" he asked, desperate to change the subject.

She took his hand in hers and tugged him along into the trees as they continued to track Gillette. "There's a panther preserve not far from here. I did the touristy thing there and learned about Sampson, how he was rescued from a circus, how he'd been abused. I kind of fell in love with him. He was so sweet and it was so sad that he couldn't fend for himself against the other panthers. He had to be kept separate. I guess I visited so much he grew attached to me. Somehow he escaped and ended up here. I walked into my apartment and he'd climbed through the window and was sitting on my couch."

Jake shook his head and held up a branch for her to walk underneath it. "That had to be scary."

"More than you realize. I screamed and scared us both. He ran out the window. It wasn't until then that I realized which cat he was, and that he was harmless and just looking for company. I figured he was hungry, too, unable to catch and eat anything himself. So I went into town the next morning and bought a meat grinder and some raw meat in case he came back. A week later he did, and he's been coming back ever since. Amy or I usually feed him once a day, but sometimes we don't see him for several days."

"It never occurred to you to call the panther preserve people and have them come pick him up?"

"Oh, sure it occurred to me. But I discarded that idea as soon as I thought of it. He was lonely there. I was lonely here. We made a great team."

He shook his head, smiling. "I think I saw him that first night. He ran across the road in front of my car. That's what made me see Gillette's car back in the woods."

"Huh. Strange."

"Or fate."

She glanced up at him, probably wondering whether he meant because he'd found the car, or her. Since he wasn't quite sure himself, he didn't say anything.

She stopped and pointed off to their right. "It's getting too dry here to show prints, but see those broken palmetto fronds? I think he ran through there. Those aren't easy to break, so he must have been in a hurry or might have even fallen down."

"Maybe Sampson was chasing him."

She laughed. "Maybe."

Twenty minutes later the trail of broken twigs and bent branches ended at the beginning of a bog.

"He couldn't have crossed this without a canoe," Faye said.

"Because it's so deep?"

"Because it's full of snakes and gators." She turned around. "I don't see a return path."

Jake immediately shoved her behind him and drew his gun. He pointed it up in the trees closest to him, squinting against the late-morning sun. "Gillette, we know you're hiding. I'm going to start shooting up into the trees if you don't come down in the next ten seconds."

Faye put her hand on his forearm. "Threatening to shoot trees again?"

He shrugged. "It worked with you. Why not with him?"

She laughed. "You don't need the gun. He's not dangerous."

Jake knew better. But at the insistent pressure of Faye's hand on his arm, he relented and lowered his gun to his side. He didn't holster it, though. There was only so far he was willing to go.

She nodded her thanks. "Calvin. It's okay. You can come down. Jake's a...friend. It's safe."

Jake looked up at the trees, studying each branch. There, about fifteen feet up the tree closest to them, he saw Gillette. Wearing jeans and a black T-shirt, he blended in almost perfectly. Jake edged his pistol hand slightly back behind his thigh so it wasn't obvious he was holding a gun if Gillette hadn't seen it earlier.

"All right," Gillette said. "I'm coming down."

He wasn't much of a tree climber, or at least, he wasn't as good at getting down as he was going up. Faye ended up talking him through it, telling him where to place each foot. By the time he reached the bottom branch, just a good five-foot jump to the ground, he was shaking so much that pine needles were falling down around him.

Faye looked to Jake for help. He couldn't have planned it any better. He sighed as if helping Gillette was an inconvenience, instead of an opportunity. He holstered his pistol before reaching up and yanking Gillette's leg. The smaller man tumbled out of the tree with a frightened shout, landing on a pile of pine needles and rolling to a stop against the base of the tree.

Faye's gasp of outrage turned to an indignant shriek when Jake tugged Gillette's hands behind him and cuffed them together before hauling him upright.

"What are you doing?" Faye demanded.

"I thought you said he was a friend," Gillette accused, aiming a glare at Jake.

"He is. He's a private investigator. Let him go, Jake."

He shoved the handcuff key in his front jeans pocket. "Sorry, Faye. I truly am." He patted Gillette down but didn't find any weapons. He forced him to sit on the forest floor. Jake put his foot on the chain between the cuffs so Gillette couldn't get up. Then he did one of the hardest things he'd ever had to do. He pulled out his pistol, and pointed it at Faye.

"Toss your gun, and your knife," he ordered. "Over there in the bushes."

Her face went pale. "Why? What are you going to do?"

He could have handled her anger. But the flash of fear in her eyes cut him deeply. "Stop looking at me like that. I'm not going to hurt you unless you draw your gun on me."

Confusion creased her brow. "I don't understand. I thought you were going to help me find Calvin, to let him know about his brother."

"I don't have a brother," Calvin said. "What are you talking about?"

"You do. The man who hired Jake to find you is your brother. When you were put in foster care, you must have had a brother and never knew it. He's trying to find you now. Isn't that right, Jake?"

He fisted his left hand beside him. "That was a cover. To get you to lead me to Gillette. The gun, Faye. And the knife. Throw them into the trees."

She aimed a wounded look at him before bending down and freeing the weapons. She tossed them into the grass. When she straightened, she wouldn't even look at him. Her face had gone hard, and was so pale it worried him.

"So much for my instincts that you were a good man," she whispered brokenly.

He winced.

"Now what?" she asked, her voice sounding wooden. "I suppose you're going to kill us. It's a good plan. No one will find our bodies out here."

Gillette jerked forward, trying to pull away. Jake shoved his shoulder and slammed him facedown onto the ground. He kneeled beside him with his knee in the middle of Gillette's back to keep him from moving.

"Enough," Jake said. "I'm not here to hurt either of you. I'm a private investigator. I didn't lie about that. I'm under contract to the FBI to find you two so you can face charges in Tuscaloosa."

Faye's brows drew down in confusion. "Charges? What charges?"

"We didn't run from any charges," Gillette insisted.

"No, but you did run. The charges were filed *in absentia.* You're both wanted for murder."

"Murder?" They both said the word at the same time and with the same degree of shock.

Either they had excellent acting skills, or they were truly surprised. A niggle of doubt swept through Jake, but he forced it away. They *had* run. Innocent people didn't run. Or use an alias, as Faye had done.

"Calvin Gillette, Faith Decker, you're both under citizen's arrest."

Faye's eyes widened at the use of her legal name. Handcuffing her was what he should do next. And he'd brought along an extra pair for that purpose. But he couldn't bring himself to do it. Dex was right after all. Faye had gotten under his skin. He'd do his job, take her in, but *he* wouldn't be the one to cuff her. Hopefully he could get a signal out here. Because taking both of them back by himself, with only one of them cuffed, could get messy. He pulled out his phone to call Holder.

"Don't," Faye said, a sense of urgency in her tone. "Please, Jake. For me. Wait. Hear us out. Something's terribly wrong here. Neither of us has killed anyone. I swear."

He steeled himself against the pleading tone of her voice. "As many times as you've lied to me, swearing doesn't hold much weight."

She flinched. "Fair enough. Looks like we've both been lying to each other, though. Was last night a lie, too?"

"Don't," he said. "Don't go there. This has nothing to do with that and you know it."

"Do I?" She looked away, but not before he saw the sparkle of unshed tears in her eyes.

*Damn it.*

He tried the phone. No service. Of course.

"We have a right to know who's trying to frame us," her broken voice called out to him. She sounded so hurt, so lost, it was torture not to go to her and pull her into his arms.

"No one's trying to frame you. I'm working for Special Agent Quinn Fugate. He's been following your case out of the Birmingham, Alabama, field office. But the crime took place in Tuscaloosa. The victim was Vincent Genovese."

"Genovese? Calvin and I *worked* for him. We didn't *kill* him."

"Don't tell him anything," Calvin warned.

"Remember the sister I told you about? My foster sister?" Faye asked. "I wasn't completely honest. It was a brother, not a sister. Calvin was the one I was talking about. He's the one I started a landscaping business with. That job I told you about, renovating gardens on a massive estate, that was Genovese's estate."

"Shut up," Calvin called out. "Don't make yourself a target, Faye."

Jake pressed his knee harder against Gillette's back. Gillette grimaced but didn't say anything else.

"Tell me what happened, Faye," Jake said.

"We'd heard rumors about Genovese, that

he might be part of organized crime. But we didn't think there could be any harm in taking the job. And we really needed that job. We were fresh out of college, broke, with student loans coming due. It was just a few months of work, and it was on the up-and-up. We were just redoing the gardens. So we took the job. And it worked out great, at first. But when you're outside all the time, you start noticing patterns, the people who come and go. You hear conversations you aren't meant to hear, see things you aren't supposed to see."

"Damn it, Faye. Shut *up*," Calvin swore.

She ignored him and started across the clearing toward Jake. He tightened his hand around the pistol and watched her warily. He couldn't let her get close enough to flip him or pull some other kind of trick. No underestimating this time. But could he pull the trigger if he had to? He honestly didn't know.

"Genovese would have us come in the house sometimes, for meetings in his front study. We'd review architectural drawings, gain approval for the garden plans. He paid us in cash out of his wall safe. That made us both uneasy, but we took it."

"Faye," Gillette cried out.

Jake leaned down close to him. "Interrupt again and I'll gag you. Go on, Faye."

She stopped and flicked a glance at Gillette. "My point is this. We knew Genovese, liked him, had no reason to hurt him. We were both working the day he was killed. Someone shot him while he was in the front study. But, Jake, you have to believe me. Calvin and I didn't pull the trigger. Someone saw the killer. There was an eyewitness."

"Quinn didn't mention that."

"That's because the person who saw Genovese get shot didn't tell the police."

Jake looked down at Gillette. He already knew what was coming. "And who is this supposed eyewitness?"

She drew a shaky breath. "Me."

# Chapter Ten

Jake was still reeling from Faye's declaration about witnessing Genovese's murder. He didn't know what to think, or what his next steps should be. The only thing he was sure of was that he wanted more details, because the sincerity in Faye's voice resonated inside him. This time she wasn't lying. He was *almost* sure of it. But then why had she and Gillette gone on the run? Why was she using an alias? Who were they hiding from?

He kept his pistol in close reach on the ground beside him where he could grab it if he needed to. He'd sat Gillette up against a tree about ten feet away. Then he and Faye had shucked their backpacks and left them in the grass before sitting down across from each other so they could talk.

"From the beginning," he said.

She braced her hands on the ground beside her. "There's not much to tell. I was planting

flowers around the base of some shrubs outside the window to Genovese's study. When I
finished, I gathered my tools and stood to go
put them in the gardening house at the back
of the property. I was facing the window and
saw Genovese arguing with another man. The
man had a gun in his hand. I froze. I couldn't
move. And then he just…shot him. I think I
must have screamed or moved or something.
The shooter jerked around and raised his gun.
I ducked down and the window cracked above
me."

Jake put his hand on hers. "He tried to shoot
you?"

"Yes. I dropped my tools and ran."

"Where were *you*?" he called out to Gillette.

"I was outside, too, on the other side of the
house. I heard the shots, and one of the maids
screaming. I ran inside and found a group of
servants standing around Genovese. One of
them had already called the police."

"Did anyone else see the shooter?"

They both shook their heads.

"Okay, what happened next? The police
came? Did you both give statements?"

"Yes," Faye said. "But I didn't tell them I
actually saw Genovese get shot."

"Why not?"

She clasped her hands together in her lap.

"I was too scared. I'd seen enough while working there to know that if I said anything I could end up dead like Genovese. The man who shot him wasn't a very nice man. We think he was into organized crime, like Genovese. Calvin and I had both seen him several times. We'd heard things, and knew he was dangerous. He always had two other men with him, bodyguards, except for that day. He must have snuck onto the property, because his car wasn't there, and neither were his men. I think he'd planned to kill Genovese. But he didn't plan on anyone seeing him. I knew I had to get out of there or he'd come back and find me. That's why we ran. As soon as the police let us go, we were gone."

The certainty in her voice, and Gillette's answering nod from the other side of the clearing, had him feeling frustrated. "But you talked to the police. You could have told them what you saw. They could have protected you."

"Like they protected her in foster care?" Gillette called out. "We know all about police protection."

Everything inside Jake froze. All kinds of horrible scenarios about what Faye might have suffered as a young girl flashed through his mind.

She entwined her fingers with his. "Don't look at me like that. It's not as bad as you think. We had some…rough times growing up. There were some…bad homes. But Calvin was always there to defend me, to protect me. I owe him so much. Even when the authorities didn't believe our claims about the abuse, or attempted abuse really, Calvin was there for me. We stuck together, defended each other. That's the only way I survived."

She pulled her hand back. "But that's not the point, is it? The point is that neither of us had any reason to trust the authorities. After Genovese died, and his killer shot that bullet at me, barely missing, Calvin and I knew we had to disappear. I came back here, to Mystic Glades. Calvin moved around a lot, eventually settling in Naples. Everything was fine until last week, when he saw one of the killer's men. He panicked and called me and was on his way here when he crashed his car."

"Who is he? The man who killed Genovese?"

"Kevin Rossi."

Jake tried to place the name, but it didn't sound familiar. Then again, he wasn't from Alabama. "Okay, okay. The problem is, if you're telling the truth, you have no proof."

"But we do. At least, we can prove *we* didn't shoot anyone. The police tested us to see if either of us had fired a gun. They tested all of us, everyone who worked on the estate."

"A GSR test, gunshot residue?"

"I believe that's what they called it, yes. We were all cleared."

Jake carefully watched both of them, looking back and forth. He wanted to believe what she was telling him. But he sensed there was something more to the story, something neither of them wanted to share.

"You said you used to come to Mystic Glades during the summers. Did you use your real name or your alias back then?"

She gave him an aggravated look. "I'm not using an alias. Faye is my nickname, and Star is my middle name. My full legal name is Faith Star Decker. To my friends, I've always been Faye Star. But on legal documents I have to use Faith Decker." She took his hand in hers again. "Jake, I'm telling the truth. Neither Calvin nor I have done anything wrong."

Jake shook his head. "Gillette is known as a petty thief in Naples."

She flashed an irritated glance at Gillette, sitting against the tree. "I'm not surprised. He's been known to stretch the law a bit more than he should. But he's not a murderer." She squeezed his hand. "If you take us to Naples, make us go to court, you could be signing our death warrant. Rossi would find us. I have a new life in Mystic Glades. And Calvin can come here, too, or start a new life somewhere else. We can be safe again. All you have to do is walk away, pretend you never met me." Her voice broke and she tugged her hands back from him. "Pretend you never met Calvin. We can both go back to our lives the way they've been for the past thirteen months."

That little catch in her voice had him wanting to pull her into his arms again. But he couldn't do that. Not yet. Things weren't as simple as she naively believed them to be.

"Faye, if I hadn't come along, someone else would have. What about all of your friends back in town? What do you think could happen to them if the mob really is looking for you and they eventually find you?"

Her lips tightened.

Jake turned his attention to Gillette. "If you were trying to find Faye when you crashed your car, why didn't you let the two men you saw in the woods in the past few days take you to her? Instead, you hid out."

"I didn't know who they were. They could have been working for the killer."

Jake swore. "This is one hell of a mess. What did you do to bring attention to yourself back in Naples? Or did you go back home, to Tuscaloosa, and got spotted there? Did you bring the FBI and Rossi back here? Faye would have been better off if you'd stayed way the hell away from her. She's not safe anymore, you've got that right. But not because of me. Because of you."

Gillette glared at him and shoved himself to his feet. Jake grabbed his pistol and jumped up at the same time as Faye.

"Stop it, both of you," she said. "None of this is resolving anything."

"You've got that right," Jake said. "The only way to fix this is for all of us to go back into town, to Naples. We'll sit with Deputy Holder and talk this out. I'll notify special agent Quinn and he can arrange for some US Marshals to come down here to protect you." He looked at Faye. "If you testify against the man you saw, and he's in organized crime, you could go into WitSec, the Witness Security Program. They'll give you a new name, a new life, and you won't have to worry anymore. You'll be safe."

She shook her head, her blond hair bouncing around her shoulders. "No. I can't do that."

"Why not?"

She shot a glance at Gillette. He looked away.

Jake grabbed her shoulders. "Am I a fool again to believe what you've been telling me?

You've lied so many times, I'm not sure what to believe. Part of me wants to buy everything you just said, but you and your 'brother' are holding out on something. You haven't told me the full story. There's obviously another reason you don't want to go to the police. What is it?"

Her eyes filled with misery. "I'm so sorry, Jake."

Her apology, and the sudden quiet in the glade, had him whirling around.

Gillette crashed into him like a small bull, knocking him to the ground. Jake swore and reached for his pistol. But it wasn't there. It was still on the ground where he and Faye had been sitting. He tried to grab Gillette, but the smaller man rolled out of the way and jumped to his feet.

A shrill whistle echoed through the clearing.

Jake looked behind him. Faye was the one who'd whistled. He braced his hands on the ground and shoved himself to his knees. Something hard crashed against him again, knocking him back down. Warm, thick fur brushed against the side of his face. Sampson had jumped on him from one of the nearby trees and had his paws wrapped around him like a blanket.

"Get off me, Sampson," Jake ordered as he tried to shake the cat off.

Another shrill whistle sounded. Sampson licked the side of Jake's neck as if in apology, then leaped off him and bounded back into the trees.

Jake jumped to his feet, then froze.

Faye stood in front of him, just out of his reach, pointing his own gun at him.

"I'm truly sorry," she said. "But you've left me no choice. Toss me the keys to the handcuffs."

"Don't do this," he said.

"I have no choice," she repeated. "The keys."

He tossed them to her.

She caught them in her left hand, her right hand never wavering as she held the gun on him. Gillette immediately sidled over to her like a snake, turning his back so she could unlock the cuffs.

"What are you going to do?" Jake asked.

"We're leaving," she said as the handcuffs dropped to the forest floor.

Gillette rubbed his wrists, aiming a glare at Jake. "Give me the gun. I'll make sure he doesn't try to follow us."

"Shut up, Calvin. You've caused enough trouble as it is," she said.

His mouth tightened but he didn't say anything else.

"You've got everything you need to survive

out here for a couple of days in your pack," she said to Jake, motioning toward where he'd set the bag earlier. "You remember the way we came. Just go back the same way. Keep the sun to your right. Don't try to travel at night. It's too dangerous. I'll leave the canoe for you. Since you won't have to go slow to search for anyone on your way back, if you hurry you could make it to Mystic Glades before dark."

"And where will you be?" he asked.

"Gone. Calvin and I will find somewhere else to hide."

"Hiding isn't the answer. Don't do this. Please."

"I'm sorry, Jake. There are things you don't understand."

"Then explain them to me. Let me help you."

She shook her head. "You can't help me. I'm in too deep. We both are. Now close your eyes."

"I'm not closing my eyes."

Gillette picked up a thick, broken piece of branch from near one of the pine trees and hefted it in his hands. "I can take care of that."

"Touch him and I'll shoot you, Calvin. I'm not joking."

He gave her an irritated look and dropped the branch.

"Close your eyes, Jake," she repeated. "Please."

He sighed heavily and closed his eyes.

"Now count to twenty before you open them again."

"This is ridiculous," he grumbled. "We're not in elementary school playing a game of hide-and-seek." He opened his eyes. Faye and Gillette were gone.

## Chapter Eleven

Jake sat on the same log he'd sat on yester-day afternoon, when he'd called Dex after he and Faye had stopped to set up camp. He'd managed to backtrack to the same spot, but he wasn't so sure about his ability to find the canoe—assuming Faye really had left it for him—and figure out how to get back to Mystic Glades. And just like yesterday, he was on the phone with Dex.

"I still can't believe I let her distract me, and Gillette got the drop on me. Stupid, stu-pid, stupid."

"No arguments here," Dex said.

"Thanks, buddy."

"Any time. So, basically, the bad guys got away, after blaming some phantom named Kevin Rossi for their crimes. We're out a boatload of money, meaning I'm going to have to pump more of *my* money into this venture to keep it afloat. And you're lost. Did I miss anything?"

"Other than the fact that you might need to pay my rent for a few months, nope. That pretty much sums it up."

Dex groaned. "You're killing me."

"You're the money man. You knew the risks when you decided to partner with me."

"In other words you don't feel sorry for me."

"I don't feel sorry for millionaires."

"Billionaire."

"No one likes a bragger."

Dex laughed.

"All these trees look the same to me. Faye did say keep the sun on my right side. But since it's noon and the sun is directly overhead, that's not too helpful."

"You want me to call search and rescue?"

"You're kidding, right? Holder called off the search at the accident site in just a few hours, and he had a good starting place for the search. If you ask him to look for me somewhere within a fifteen-mile radius of Mystic Glades, he'll probably laugh you off the phone. No one seems to even know where Mystic Glades is except the people who live there."

"Sounds like an awesome place."

"You have no idea." He picked up a rock and tossed it at a dark spot near a tree. When nothing moved, he relaxed, a little. Maybe that *wasn't* a gator hiding under the bushes. Then again, maybe it was, and it was waiting for him to come a little closer. The whole area was giving him the creeps. He was seeing predators everywhere he looked.

"Seriously, man. You need me to call the cops?" Dex asked.

If the person who'd stranded him out here had been anyone but Faye, he'd say yes. But telling the police she'd left him here could make things worse for her, if that was even possible. He didn't want her hit with more charges.

Gillette was the true one to blame. He was a bad influence on Faye. He'd protected her when they were younger, which made her feel obligated to protect him now. Whatever the two of them were *really* running from could be laid at Gillette's door. Jake would bet his last bullet on it.

"Don't call the cops yet. I'll make a go of trying to find my way back. I've done okay so far. She left me the backpack. I've got plenty of food and water. And a tent if I don't make it back tonight. She even left my gun, which was a surprise. Obviously she wasn't trying to leave me defenseless out here."

Dex snorted. "No, she just left a townie in

the middle of the wild, knowing he probably will never find his way out. Those supplies won't last forever. Neither will the battery on your phone."

"I've got a solar charger or it wouldn't have lasted this long. Not that it works in more than a handful of places out here anyway. The cell service is ridiculous. But I'm okay. For now. Tell me what you've found out since our last chat."

"Nothing surprising." A keyboard tapped in the background as Dex went to work on his computer. "Okay, first, I decided to look at Quinn, just to set your mind at ease. He's exactly who he says he is—a special agent with the FBI on the verge of retirement. And his record is as good as he boasted. There's hardly a blemish on it, except for Genovese. That case went cold within hours of the murder. Quinn's story that he was hiring us on the side because the Bureau wouldn't pump any more money into the case seems accurate. He really just wants a clear record when he retires."

"Okay. Why was the FBI involved in the Genovese case in the first place? It was just a murder, if there is such a thing as 'just' a murder."

"Good question. I wondered the same thing and dug in a bit. Because of Genovese's occupation as resident mob guy and head of organized crime in Tuscaloosa and everything within a fifty-mile radius, he was already under investigation by the FBI. They were trying to break into his operation for a couple of years before his death, trying to get a guy on the inside, although I couldn't get any details on that. Quantico wasn't pleased when Genovese got whacked. They were left with nothing after spending considerable resources on him. They decided to cut their losses and move on, which is why they left the murder investigation to the locals. Not that *they* did much, either. Genovese didn't have any family to push them to keep the case open. All his assets went to charity. No one seems to care about finding his murderer."

"Except Quinn."

"Except Quinn, yes. If he solves the murder, it doesn't rehabilitate the case against the mob the FBI was going for, but at least he ties up the loose ends and can get credit for solving the murder. For someone with a twenty-five-year career, something like that can be pretty important, I would imagine."

Jake rubbed the ache starting between his eyes. "Okay, did you find anything else about Faye and Gillette?"

"Not much more than we knew when we

started. I did confirm they both basically grew up in foster care together. And I may have bribed a clerk at UA to give me the name of one of Faye's roommates so I could ask her some questions."

"Bribed, huh?"

"Looks like I'm flying to Tuscaloosa for dinner when this case is wrapped up."

Jake laughed. "I hope she's worth it."

"She sounded gorgeous on the phone."

He laughed again. "I'm sure she is. What did you find out?"

"The roomie said Faye basically had two really good friends—Amber Callahan and our friend Gillette. Faye didn't open up much to her, but the roomie said Faye was really tight with Gillette. He got into trouble, petty, stupid stuff. And she was always there to bail him out, sometimes literally. He has a record, most of it juvenile types of crimes. I got the impression Faye was like a mother hen, or even a bulldog when it came to being loyal to him."

Jake thought back to the incredible night he'd spent with her, and then how quickly she'd turned on him to save Calvin. He laughed bitterly. "Yeah, you didn't have to tell me that. I know where her loyalty lies." Certainly not with him. He kicked at a dried branch lying near the log, smashing it in two.

"Is there something else you're not telling me about what happened out there?" Dex asked.

"Nothing I'm going to share."

"O…kay. We'll just move along then. Assuming you can find your way out of there without me calling in the troops, what's our next course of action? Should I get Holder to put out a BOLO for Gillette and Star?"

Jake stood and did a slow turn again, making sure he wasn't about to become prey to something sneaking up behind him, before sitting back down on the log. "I wouldn't have a clue what to tell them to be on the lookout for. Gillette, as far as I know, doesn't have another car out here anywhere. And Faye didn't have one at her shop. For all I know, they're escaping by canoe or on foot. And knowing Faye, I don't see her going down the highway back to civilization. She'll take advantage of her knowledge of the Everglades and come out the other side, probably south of here, closer to the Big Cypress Preserve or the Tamiami Trail."

"Then we're just going to do, what, nothing?"

"You can look into Rossi."

"The phantom killer. Waste of time, but okay. Back to my original question. What else are we going to do, if anything?"

"Give me a minute." He scrubbed the stubble

on his face that he hadn't shaved because he'd forgotten to bring his razor. He wasn't coming up with any amazing strategies, so he decided to play it by the book, to work it the way he would if he was undercover as a detective in Saint Augustine. And he'd use his knowledge of Faye to guide him—assuming he ever made it back to civilization and found her. "Okay. This is what we're going to do."

After listening to Jake's plan, Dex said, "That's it? That's the brilliance you came up with?"

"You got something better?"

"No. But I haven't been a police detective for the past ten years, either."

"Bite me."

Dex laughed and ended the call.

With a rough plan in place, he shoved his phone back in his pocket. He stood and looked around again, trying to get his bearings, trying to remember where he and Faye had emerged from the trees yesterday before going back in where they made camp. He considered himself to be observant. He'd been trained to remember things like hair color, height, approximate weight, even the clothing someone was wearing. He could look at a crowd of people for just a few seconds and remember how many men and women were in the crowd, even the mix of ethnicity, all as part of his training as a police officer. But remembering which clump of trees he and Faye had walked through was an entirely different skill set he apparently did not possess.

The sun was still high overhead, which meant he had several hours of false starts if necessary before he lost the light and had to give up for the night. Might as well start right now.

He picked what he thought might be the right direction and headed out. A few hours later, he was back in the exact same spot, cursing whoever had come up with that saying that lost people often went in circles. *He* certainly had. He took a deep sip of water, shoved the bottle back in his pack, then started out in what he hoped was the *real* right direction. Again.

"Don't go that way unless you want to walk to Key West," a soft voice called out.

He drew his gun and whirled around. Faye stood about twenty feet behind him, her expression a mixture of sadness and regret as she slowly lifted her hands in the air.

FAYE STOOD INSIDE her bedroom, relieved to be clean and dressed in a fresh blue skirt and top, but not at all pleased she would have to knock on her own door for Jake to let her out. Not that she could blame him for shoving a chair up under the handle so she wouldn't disappear again while they both took showers. He was furious with her for letting Calvin go and had barely spoken on the trip back to Mystic Glades.

He was waging a war within himself about what to do with her. He'd admitted that the policeman inside him wanted to call Deputy Holder and the FBI agent who'd hired him and have her arrested. But he hadn't. Not yet. She suspected, she hoped, the part he wasn't telling her was that the lover she'd shared herself with didn't want to turn her in. He *did* seem surprised and confused over why she'd come back for him.

The answer to that was easy. She couldn't have lived with herself if something had happened because she'd abandoned him in the swamp. She couldn't have done that to anyone, but especially not to Jake. Somehow he'd managed to work his way past her defenses to the point where she was willing to risk her life just by being with him, when she should have been running somewhere safe as Calvin was doing at this very moment.

She smoothed her skirts, flipped her hair

back behind her shoulders and knocked on the door. Boots echoed on the hardwood floor from the living room. The chair on the other side scraped against wood before he opened the door.

He braced his arms against the frame. Neither of them said anything for a moment, facing off like the adversaries they'd become.

"You hungry?" he asked, his voice sounding strained.

The suggestion of food elicited an immediate growl from her stomach. She slapped her hand against her belly. "Apparently I am."

His lips curved in an *almost* smile. After this morning, she was grateful for that much at least.

He stepped back and waved his hand toward her eat-in kitchen. A mixed salad sat in the middle of the table. Sandwiches sat on a plate beside it.

"Based on the frightening lack of meat in your refrigerator," he said, "I'm guessing you're a vegetarian of some kind. All I could find for sandwiches was cheese. But it's better than beef jerky and granola bars. Hopefully."

"I eat cheese sandwiches all the time. It looks great. Thank you."

He surprised her by pulling out her chair for her before taking his own seat. Since both of them had skipped lunch and dinner in their rush to get back to Mystic Glades before nightfall, they were both hungry and ate quickly. Faye didn't mind. It meant no stilted conversation and that she could eat without being grilled with dozens of questions. But as soon as she finished her last bite and put her fork down, Jake did the same, as if he'd been going through the motions of eating just until she was done.

With both of them helping, the cleanup went fast. Too fast. Soon there was nothing left to do except sit on the couch and start the interrogation.

They both sat sideways, facing each other.

"Go ahead," she said. "Get it over with. Ask your questions."

"What's the real reason you came back for me?" he asked. "What's the catch?"

She stiffened. "No catch. I never intended to leave you stranded. As soon as Calvin was safe, I went looking for you."

"Again, why?"

If he couldn't figure out that she cared about him, she sure wasn't going to tell him. "Because you're a human being. I wouldn't leave anyone out there to fend for themselves. It wouldn't be right."

His eyes searched hers, as if he could divine the truth. "That's the only reason?"

"Of course. What other reason would there be?"

His mouth tightened, making her wonder what he'd expected her to say.

"Where's Gillette?"

"Gone, where no one will find him."

He cursed and shook his head. "He's a fugitive, Faye. He needs to face up to his past."

"We're both fugitives, according to you. But neither of us has done anything wrong."

He put his hands on her shoulders and pulled her toward him. "Faye, I found him once. I'll find him again. But if you help me, it would make things easier on you. I can tell the Feds you cooperated. That might help your own case."

She tugged his hands off her shoulders and sat back. "Make things easier on me? In case you haven't figured it out yet, that's not the kind of person I am. I don't hurt other people so I can take the easy way out."

He blew out a frustrated breath. "You went to college for four years. You had a future ahead of you, and you gave it up to hide out in Mystic Glades. I don't buy your fear of policemen as the only answer. There's something more. What did you and Calvin do that makes you too afraid to go to the cops even though you think a killer might be looking for you?"

When she didn't answer, his brows drew down like a dark cloud. "Faye, I can help you. But you have to trust me. You have to open up to me."

"By telling you where Calvin is? So you can have him arrested for a crime he didn't commit?" She shook her head, her lip curling with disgust. "We may not be blood-related siblings, but I have more loyalty to him than that. I would never trade my safety for his. I thought you would understand that since you knew what it was like to lose your only sibling."

He winced as if she'd hit him, immediately making her regret her harsh words. But what was done was done. She needed to convince him to leave so she could leave, too. She was trying to put a brave face on everything, but in reality, she was terrified. Her past had already caught up to her, and she had to get out of here before it was too late.

It wasn't that she didn't trust Jake to help her. She believed he'd do everything he could if she let him. But that would only put him in danger. And even though she wasn't a murderer, she wasn't completely innocent. If he found out what she *had* done, he'd have to make a choice.

And she was very much afraid that keeping her secret was a choice he wouldn't make.

He sat there a long time, watching her, perhaps waiting for her to change her mind. But she'd already made up her mind. Nothing could make her risk Jake's life to help her out of a mess of her own making. He deserved better than that.

Finally, he stood. And without another word, he left the apartment.

She blinked in surprise. Was he letting her go then? She ran to the window at the end of the living room and looked down into the street. Moments later, Jake's black Charger turned out of the side alley beside her store, out onto the main drag. He didn't look up at the window as he drove by. And soon, he passed through the gates of Mystic Glades and disappeared from sight.

She sank down to the floor, stunned. He was letting her go. Tears pricked the backs of her eyes. *He's letting me go.* He'd forced his way into her life, into her heart, and he was letting her go. She wrapped her arms around her knees, and for the first time in a very long time, she stopped being strong, stopped trying to bottle up her frustrations, her fears, her regrets. The tears flowed freely, branding hot tracks down her cheeks and falling to the floor.

A long time later, when the room had gone dark around her, she drew a shaky breath. She went into the bathroom and washed her face. She was ashamed that she'd allowed herself to sit there so long feeling sorry for herself. She didn't have time for that. Staying here was no longer an option. The past had caught up to her and Calvin.

They'd had a terrible fight after leaving Jake in the swamp, the same fight they'd had several times over the past few months. Her answer to his question remained the same as it always had—no. He'd been furious, but there was nothing he could do about her decision. She took him to a friend's cabin near the highway. The last she saw of Calvin, he was staring at her from the passenger seat as Eddie drove him back to Naples to collect his things. The plan was for Calvin to get a bus ticket and find his own place for a new start. A few months from now, when they were both settled and Calvin's anger cooled, they'd contact each other through email and reconnect. They'd both apologize and everything would be fine. That was the constant cycle of their relationship.

She sighed and started packing another one of her backpacks. Eddie had been insistent that she didn't need to pay him for taking Calvin to Naples. But he didn't make much money and she knew he couldn't afford the gas. Since neither she nor Calvin had cash on them, she'd promised to return later. She would stop at Eddie's place first, then continue south to the Tamiami Trail. Maybe she'd keep going all the way to the Florida Keys. It was probably beautiful this time of year. And she could probably get a job waiting tables at any number of tourist traps down there. It wouldn't be her beloved Everglades, but she could think of worse things than living near the ocean every day.

Since she couldn't be sure that Jake wouldn't change his mind and come back, possibly bringing the police with him, she couldn't risk taking the extra time to say goodbye to her friends. She'd have to tell Amy, of course, since she took care of the shop. And she'd have to make sure Amy continued to feed Sampson every day. But other than that, it was time to go.

The grief over leaving her friends, and leaving Mystic Glades, clogged her throat. But she couldn't give in. She had to hurry.

She hid another knife in the sheath sewn into the folds of her skirts. The knife and pistol Jake had made her toss back in the woods had ended up somewhere in the muddy bog. She hadn't taken the time to try to find them.

She regretted that now. Hopefully she wouldn't get into a tight spot where she needed a gun.

Her money situation wasn't great, but thanks to the generosity of her "adopted" Callahan family, she'd be okay for several months before she'd start getting desperate. By then, hopefully she'd have a new job—one that paid cash under the table and didn't require a Social Security number.

She took one last look around, then headed downstairs.

JAKE HAD TAKEN a gamble. Based on Faye's pattern, he was assuming she would run again after he left. The gamble was that he was betting she wouldn't be watching out the window for his car to turn around and drive back through the main entrance of Mystic Glades. As soon as he'd driven back inside, he'd turned a sharp left and parked his car behind one of the other businesses off the main road, a bookstore called Between the Covers.

He hopped out and hurried back toward The Moon and Star, keeping to the backs of the shops, close to the tree line. He'd just tucked himself behind a thick live oak behind Faye's store when the back door opened. She stood in the doorway with Amy. They said something to each other and hugged. Faye had her backpack on, and from the tears streaming down Amy's face, it was obvious Faye had no intention of coming back.

She jogged to the edge of the trees, only ten feet from where Jake stood watching her. She waved at Amy and disappeared with a flick of her deep blue skirts.

# Chapter Twelve

Faye was moving fast, so fast that Jake had a hard time keeping up with her. Not that he couldn't outrun her. His legs were much longer than hers. But to make his way through the unfamiliar terrain of the Everglades, at night, without getting stuck in a bog or crashing through the low-hanging tree limbs and alerting her of his presence slowed him down far more than he'd anticipated. Hopefully he'd catch her before she got so far ahead that he couldn't hear her.

He followed her for over two hours, something he couldn't have done if the moon wasn't so bright. But then again, if the moon wasn't bright tonight he'd have never let her take off into the woods. He'd have had to come up with a new plan.

She rarely stopped to catch her breath. He was usually gasping for air by the time she did.

He considered himself to be in excellent shape, but he wasn't in the habit of running marathons.

There were a couple of times when he lost her and started to panic. But since she obviously didn't think anyone was following her, she made no attempt to be quiet or disguise her tracks. He watched for broken branches and footprints as she'd done when they'd been searching for Gillette together, and he was able to pick up her trail again.

When they started on their third hour, everything suddenly went silent. Jake hurried forward until he could see her and ducked behind some bushes. Thirty feet ahead, she stood in what appeared to be as much of a yard as one could have out in the marsh. In front of her was a tiny building, one of the smallest houses Jake had ever seen. But it was well kept, with a lean-to on the side that sheltered the car parked there. She looked around, as if to make sure she was alone, before knocking on the door.

"It's Faye, Eddie," she said. "Can I come in?"

A full minute went by. No one opened the door. She knocked again and tried the doorknob. The door cracked open a few inches.

"Eddie?" she called, before stepping inside and closing the door.

Who the hell was Eddie? Was Calvin in there with him?

Jake checked his phone, hoping to call Dex again and give him an update. But unsurprisingly, there wasn't any service.

A scream sounded from inside the house.

Jake vaulted over a bush and sprinted for the door, pulling his pistol as he went. The door burst open just as he reached it. Faye ran outside, practically knocking him down as she barreled into him.

He grabbed her arms, steadying her. "What's wrong? Are you hurt?"

She blinked, her shock at seeing him overriding the shock of whatever she'd just seen. Her brow wrinkled in confusion. "Jake? What are you doing here?"

He lightly shook her. "Are you hurt? You screamed."

Her eyes widened. "Oh my God. Eddie. Someone...someone killed Eddie."

He grabbed her wrist and pulled her behind him toward the door.

"No, I'm not going back in there." She tugged, trying to free herself.

"And I'm not leaving you alone out here. We're sticking together. I won't let anything happen to you. Come on."

She swallowed hard and allowed him to pull her inside. He quickly cleared the main room, checking behind the couch and chair, the only places big enough for anyone to hide. The tiny kitchen to the left was completely open. There weren't any doors on the cabinets. He shut the front door and locked it before shoving her down on the floor beneath the window.

"Don't move. I mean it, Faye. Don't go outside, and don't move from this spot. Promise me. And for once, mean what you say."

Her shoulders stiffened, just as he'd intended. He'd insulted her to get her angry, to snap her out of the shock she was sliding into.

"I won't go anywhere," she bit out. "Promise."

Hoping she really was telling the truth, he swung his pistol out in front of him and headed into the tiny hallway. To his left was a bathroom, empty. He steeled himself for what he was about to find in the only other room. He crouched down, and kicked the door open. It slammed against the wall as he ran inside, sweeping his pistol back and forth.

Ignoring the gory scene on the bed since the man there posed no threat, he checked the closet and beneath the bed before holstering his gun. There wasn't any point in checking the man's pulse. He didn't have one. His throat was slit from ear to ear.

Jake pressed his finger against one of the man's wrists just because it was one of the few places not covered in blood. Warm. Which meant the killer might still be close by. He tried his phone again as he headed back into the main room. Still no service. He put it away and knelt down in front of Faye.

"Did you see anyone else when you arrived?" He gently swept her hair out of her eyes.

"No. No one. Just you. *After.*" She shuddered and pressed her hand to her throat as if struggling not to gag.

He nudged her chin up to get her to look at him. "You didn't kill Genovese."

Her eyes widened. "You believe me now?"

"Yes. You would have thrown up all over the crime scene. You don't have it in you to kill anyone."

"You picked a great time to start believing me."

He smiled sadly. "Sorry about that. Sometimes we city slickers can be a little slow. Who was Eddie?"

She gagged again and clapped her hands over her mouth.

Jake grabbed her and ran with her to the kitchen, reaching the sink just in time. He held her hair back from her face as she retched over and over, until there was nothing left in her stomach to throw up.

"Deep breaths, baby," he said. "Slow, deep breaths."

She gave him a startled look. He realized what he'd just said. Calling her "baby" wasn't exactly keeping his professional distance.

He sighed and grabbed the towel hanging from the stove handle. He wet it beneath the faucet and handed it to her. While she washed her face and rinsed her mouth, he made another quick circuit around the room, hoping to find a landline so he could call the police. There wasn't one.

Faye met up with him in the middle of the main room. "You followed me here?"

"Yes." There was no point in denying it.

"I should have expected that." She looked toward the bedroom and shuddered again. "I won't fight you anymore. I'll go with you into town, tell the police everything I know."

"Why? Why now? Because of Eddie?"

"Yes, because of Eddie. He didn't have any enemies, nothing of value to steal. He's dead because of me, because I thought I could outrun my past. But obviously I can't. And I can't risk anyone else getting hurt. I'll turn myself in."

If she'd told him that a few days ago, he'd have jumped at her offer. But suddenly *he* was the one who was hesitant. He wanted nothing more than to grab her in his arms and carry her somewhere far, far away. Where she wouldn't

Pickering Public Library
pickeringlibrary.ca

## Items that you have checked out

Title: His secretly pregnant Cinderella /
ID    33081700204606
**Due: May 5, 2022**

Title: Missing in the glades /
ID    33081500147245
**Due: May 5, 2022**

Title: Nine months to claim her /
ID    33081700142640
**Due: May 5, 2022**

Total items: 3
Account balance: $0.00
2022-04-14 9:47 AM
Checked out: 6
Overdue: 0
Hold requests: 0
Ready for pick up: 0

Thank you for using the Pickering Public Library
Automated Phone Renewal 905-831-8209
Central Branch 905-831-6265

have to face the ugliness of being arrested and going through a trial. Where he wouldn't have to worry about whether she was adequately protected if Rossi came looking for her.

For that matter, Rossi could be outside right now, waiting for her to come back out.

Jake tugged her over to the couch and pressed her down on the cushion. He sat beside her and took her hands in his.

"How does Eddie figure into this? What's his connection to you and Gillette?"

"This morning, when Calvin and I got away from you, I brought him here. I asked Eddie for a favor, to take Calvin to a bus station. Calvin insisted on going to his apartment first. He said he had to grab some of his things. After that he'd go to the station by himself, go somewhere far away and lie low for a while. But Eddie can't...couldn't...afford the gas for a trip like that. He doesn't have much money. So I told him I'd stop here tonight and reimburse him for a tank. That's all. There's no other connection."

"Calvin went back to his apartment? Didn't he say that he saw one of Rossi's thugs prowling around Naples days ago? That's why he left in the first place, right?"

Her eyes widened in dismay. "Yes. He'd left in a hurry, though. So he didn't have many of his belongings with him. I didn't think about him being in danger going back. He was just supposed to run in and out, a fast trip. Do you think someone might have been watching his apartment?"

"I think it's a real possibility."

She jumped up from the couch. Jake stood in front of her, in case she tried to go out the door.

"We have to get out of here," she said. "We have to warn him. There's a good spot for cell service about three miles north of here. If you can…get Eddie's keys, we can drive there. We can call the police from there, too."

"All right. Wait here and I'll check Eddie's pockets for the keys."

"Faye," a voice called from outside. "Get out here."

"That's Calvin!" She stepped around Jake.

He grabbed her before she could run to the door. "Wait. Let me talk to him first."

Her brows creased. "Why?"

"Because we're in a secluded area, with one dead body and three live ones. And since neither you nor I killed Eddie, do the math."

She glared up at him. "Calvin didn't do this."

"Humor me. Let me check out the situation first."

She crossed her arms and plopped back down on the couch. "Go ahead."

He flattened himself against the wall and

peeked out through the blinds. Relief shot through him as he viewed the scene outside. For once, one of his plans was working out. Not exactly the way he'd planned, but he'd take it. Unfortunately, Faye wasn't going to be happy when she realized what had happened.

He crossed to the door and pulled it open. "Come on. Let's go."

"I thought you wanted to talk to him first."

"I've seen what I need to see. It's safe."

Confusion warred with relief on her face as she hurried out the door with him. Guilt reared its ugly head again as Jake watched her eyes widen in shock. He hated that she was upset. But at least the worst was over. She was safe now. That was what mattered.

Calvin stood ten feet away, his hands tied in front of him with a white nylon rope. Another length of rope circled his waist, like a long leash. And behind him, holding the other end of that leash, with a rifle pointed at Gillette's back, was Quinn Fugate.

"It's good to see you, Quinn," Jake said. "Dex called you?"

"Yes, he did. Early this afternoon. I got into Naples just a little while ago. I was going to go straight to that Mystic Glades place Dex told me about. But I stopped by Gillette's apartment first. Guess who showed up? I followed him out here and, well, you can see what happened." He flicked the end of the rope.

Gillette stumbled but righted himself. He swore beneath his breath.

"Oh my God, oh no, oh no," Faye whispered, from behind Jake. She tugged on his shirt.

He turned back to look at her. She was shaking, pale, even worse than when she'd seen Eddie.

He was shocked at how terrified she looked. Then it dawned on him why she was so scared. Regret shot through him. "Honey, it's okay. I'm sorry. I know how bad this must look. But it's okay. The man who has Calvin tied up is an FBI agent. That's Quinn Fugate. Everything's okay. Calvin isn't in any danger."

She shook her head violently back and forth. "That's not Quinn. That's Kevin Rossi, the man I saw shoot Genovese."

# Chapter Thirteen

"Toss the pistol," Quinn ordered.

Jake reluctantly pitched his gun into a group of palmetto bushes a few feet away. Faye started around him as if to run to Gillette. He grabbed her, forcing her behind him.

"Don't move," he ordered.

"I have to do something," she whispered. "He's going to kill Calvin."

"Making yourself a target isn't the answer." He looked over his shoulder at her, waiting until she gave him a reluctant nod before facing Quinn again. "What's this all about? You hired me to find these two. Job done. All we have to do now is go into town and work on that extradition order."

Quinn laughed harshly. "Did you think I didn't hear Miss Decker tell you I was Kevin Rossi? You can drop the act. We all know I'm the one who killed Genovese. He and I had a professional disagreement that unfortunately couldn't be settled any other way."

"Professional disagreement?" Jake asked, stalling for time as he tried to think of a way to end this without anyone getting killed. Unfortunately, nothing was coming to mind.

"Playing dumb isn't your forte, Mr. Young. Obviously I was playing both sides of the fence, undercover for the FBI supposedly trying to get the goods on Genovese, while at the same time forcing Genovese to sock away money in a special account for my retirement. It was working beautifully until my boss started demanding results. I had to end the arrangement and cover my tracks. Still, even then, everything would have been fine except that Miss Decker was in the wrong place at the wrong time, and she and Mr. Gillette stuck their noses where they didn't belong. Now I'm forced to remedy the situation."

*Stuck their noses where they didn't belong?* Obviously there was still more to the Genovese story that Faye hadn't told him. Which put him at a disadvantage. It was tough to bluff or negotiate his way out of the situation if he didn't know the facts. He curled his fists in frustration. "Why now? You got away clean."

"Clean? Not exactly. These two took something that belonged to me the day they ran away. It's a ticking time bomb. I've been agonizing over it ever since, worrying it would surface some day and destroy me. Thanks to Mr. Gillette's stupidity, using an old credit card of his in Naples, I finally got a lead. But my boss is already suspicious of me, so I couldn't follow up on my own. Thanks to you, Mr. Young, I can be in and out of here and log just a couple of sick days back at the office. No one will be the wiser and I can finally retire without worrying." He flicked the rope in his hand like a whip.

Calvin grimaced when the rope snapped against his back. He stumbled forward a few steps. "He wants the journal, Faye. You have to give it to him or he's going to kill me."

Her fingers curled into the top of Jake's pants.

"What journal?" Jake asked. "What makes you think either of them have it?"

Quinn pointed his rifle at Jake again. "While I appreciate that you found these two for me, that's where your usefulness ends. Did you think it was a coincidence that I hired an investigator new to the area, with no family ties? If something happens to you, no one's going to be crying over it and pushing for an in-depth investigation. So if I were you, I'd *shut up.*"

He swung his rifle back toward Calvin. "The journal, Miss Decker. Where is it?"

"It's not here. But I can get it for you," she called out.

"Where, *exactly*, is it? In that little town of yours, Mystic something or other?"

"It's hidden in the swamp, a full day's hike from here," she said.

"Step out where I can see you." Quinn's voice was calm, cold. His gun hand was just as steady as his voice.

"No," Jake said.

The rifle jerked back toward him. Jake swore and grabbed Faye, diving to cover her just as the rifle boomed through the clearing. The shot kicked up dirt just inches from where they'd been standing. He glared at Quinn.

"That wasn't necessary," Jake growled.

"I disagree. Help her up and push her over here beside her cohort or I'll shoot again. And this time I won't miss."

"Get ready to run," Jake whispered to Faye. "When I stand up, run to the trees as fast as you can. I'll draw his fire."

"No! He'll kill you. And I can't leave Calvin."

He helped her to her feet. "Just do it. Trust me."

But instead of running, she moved away

from him just as Quinn had ordered, flashing Jake an apologetic look.

*Damn it.* He knew she meant well, that she thought she was protecting both him and her brother. But she'd just made everything that much harder. Now Quinn had three clear targets instead of two.

"Thank you, Miss Decker," Quinn said. "Your cooperation is noted and appreciated. I assume you have a cell phone, Mr. Young. Toss it to me."

He pulled his phone out and pitched it squarely at Quinn's chest, hoping he'd lose his grip on the rifle trying to catch or deflect it. But the phone hit him and dropped to the ground. The rifle didn't move. His mouth twitched with amusement.

"Good try." He stomped his heel on the phone, crushing the display.

"A day's walk to the journal. Is that correct, Miss Decker? Or are you making up stories?"

"I'm telling the truth. I hid it in a hunting cabin deep in the swamp."

"Hmm. Not the most ideal of situations, considering I don't know this area. And I certainly don't want to trek through a filthy swamp to find the thing. But then again, that's why I have leverage." He flicked the rope again. Calvin grimaced.

"I'll be generous. I'll give you twenty-four hours to retrieve it and meet us back here. If you aren't back by this time tomorrow night, with the journal, Calvin dies. If I see any signs of law enforcement poking around, or hear any chatter on the police channels—about me, the journal or anything remotely suspicious in the area—Calvin dies. If you do *anything* to alert anyone or try to get help, he dies. Understood?"

She nodded and held her hands up in a conciliatory gesture. "I understand. Please, don't hurt him. We'll get the journal."

Quinn's brows quirked up. "We? You said *you* know where the journal is. Did anyone else help you hide it?"

"No, I buried it, months ago when I first got here."

"Then you can *unbury* it by yourself." The rifle boomed. The bullet slammed into Jake, sweeping him off his feet. White-hot pain flashed through his body. His lungs seized in his chest. He crashed to the ground, his head cracking against the hard earth. The last sound he heard was Faye screaming.

JAKE RESTED ON the floor in Eddie's main room. He didn't know which was worse—his throbbing headache, the sharp jabs of pain every time Faye pressed her wet cloth against the lump on the side of his head, or the weight and chill of an ice pack sitting on top of his bruised ribs.

"Quinn?" he asked.

"Gone." She pressed the cloth against a particularly sensitive spot, making him wince.

"I'm okay. You can stop now." He pulled her hand away from his head.

"Thank God you were wearing a bullet-proof vest." She feathered her hands over his bare skin as if still searching for a bullet hole between his ribs.

"Bullet-resistant. Not bulletproof. But it still packs a punch."

"Do you think your ribs are cracked?"

"All I know is they hurt like hell."

She repositioned the ice pack against his side. He sucked in a sharp breath.

"Sorry, sorry." She dropped the ice pack to the floor and pressed the wet cloth against his head again, sending another sharp jab of pain shooting through his skull. "You've lost a lot of blood. Do you feel light-headed? Can you breathe okay? If you have a broken rib and it punctured a lung—"

He winced and grabbed her hands. "Stop worrying. I'm breathing fine and the bleeding has mostly stopped. I never would have given much credence to your woo-woo science before, but I have new respect for the pouch of medicine you carry on your necklace."

She frowned at him. "Woo-woo science? Maybe I shouldn't have wasted my very scientific powder on you after all." She tugged her hands away and plopped the cloth on the floor beside the ice pack.

He pulled her hand back to his mouth and pressed a quick kiss on it. "I didn't mean to criticize your woo-woo science. Thank you for helping me."

She rolled her eyes. "You're welcome."

"How did you manage to get me into the house?"

"Leverage and physics. I rolled you onto a blanket and used it to drag you inside. It wasn't that hard really, except for getting you over the threshold. I think I may have bumped your head a few extra times doing that. Sorry." She bit her bottom lip in sympathy.

"I'm pretty sure the threshold isn't what's making my head throb right now. Remind me again what exactly happened."

"We need to get you to a doctor. Your memory is pathetic."

"My memory is bound to be fuzzy since I was knocked unconscious." He tried to sit up. Faye braced her shoulder beneath his and helped him scoot his back against the wall with his knees drawn up in front of him.

"Thanks." He winced. "You said that Quinn had left. Are you sure he's gone?"

"I heard his car going down the road back toward the highway. And he didn't stop me when I was pulling you in here. So, yeah, I'm sure."

"The last I remember," he said, "Quinn was asking about a journal. What was he talking about?"

"Can we discuss this later, after we get you to a hospital? We'll take Eddie's car. And…" She swallowed hard. "Then we'll go to the police and report Eddie's murder, and tell them about Quinn and Calvin."

"I may not remember everything, but I'm pretty sure Quinn would have said something about *not* going to the police. I doubt he's going to make exceptions for hospitals, too. We can't risk your brother's life by outright defiance against his instructions."

She sat back on her heels. "You're right. He said no cops or he'd kill Calvin. He gave us twenty-four hours to get the journal and bring it back here."

"Then we need to get the journal. *After* you tell me what it is."

She cocked her head, studying him. "I don't understand. Why would you, a cop, even consider *not* calling the police in this situation? I would have expected that to be the first thing you'd want to do."

His mouth thinned. "I know what it's like to lose a sibling. And I also remember the cold, dead look in Quinn's eyes. He's not bluffing when he says he'll kill your brother if we don't follow his instructions. Faye?"

"Yes?"

"The journal?"

She sighed. "It's stupid. I told you earlier that Genovese paid our wages in cash from a safe in his study. Well, Calvin apparently paid a little more attention than I did to the lock combination Genovese used when he opened the safe in front of us."

"I think I know where this is heading. After the shooting, Calvin took something out of the safe before the police got there."

"A leather-bound journal."

"Stealing from a mobster isn't the smartest thing he could have done. Even a dead mobster. No telling who else might be interested in whatever's in that journal."

"I know, I know. It's been a constant source of arguments between Calvin and me ever since. I didn't discover what he'd done until we were on the run. By then it was too late to return it without associating our name with the journal. I was afraid that whoever is listed in it would come after us."

"What exactly does it contain?"

"Initials, dollar amounts, dates, account numbers, descriptions of agreements and deals. Pages and pages full of things like that. At the back there's some kind of index written in code. I'm pretty sure it's the key to figuring out the names that go with the initials."

He whistled. "Sounds to me like you've got a gold mine the FBI would love to get its hands on. Did you make any copies?"

"No. I just wanted it gone. And I was afraid Calvin would try to use it to blackmail some of the people in the journal, which would have made everything worse. So I stole it from him and hid it. I wanted to destroy it, but honestly, it seemed too important to destroy. I worried something might happen later on and we'd need it. Thank God I kept it."

"It would have been better if you'd turned it over to the police in the first place."

"Easy to say now. Obviously I didn't think so at the time."

"Sorry. I'm not trying to place blame. Let's just get it and figure out our next steps."

"Are you sure we shouldn't go to the police?"

"If we do, and Calvin pays the price, I don't want to bear that burden the rest of my life.

Let's at least start out doing what Quinn said, to buy some time until we can figure out a plan. Okay?"

She leaned in and pressed a soft kiss against his lips. "Okay."

He motioned to his shirt and vest lying a few feet away. "Put the vest on and I'll fasten the straps."

"Uh, no. Not happening. That's *yours*. You're the one who's going to wear it."

"Faye, with Quinn out there somewhere, I'm not about to wear a Kevlar vest while you have nothing to protect you. That's not even negotiable. And we're wasting time we don't have arguing about it."

She shot him an exasperated look and tossed him his shirt while she grabbed the vest. A few minutes later, he was trying to hold back his laughter as she glared at him.

"It's too big. I can hardly move in this thing." The vest extended several inches past her shoulders, practically swallowing her. It hung almost to her knees. "There's no way I can hike through the marsh like this. It's more of a hazard than protection. I can't wear it."

He grudgingly agreed and put the vest back on. He felt like a heel, but there was no sense in neither of them wearing it. Hopefully it wouldn't come to a gunfight so it wouldn't matter. He didn't bother putting it under his shirt this time. He just strapped it on over the top.

He reached for the holster on his hip. Empty. "My gun, did Quinn leave it where I threw it in the bushes?"

"Unfortunately, no. He took it with him. And he took my weapons, too, even my pocketknife I had stowed inside my backpack."

"What about Eddie? Don't all of you marsh-people have guns all over the place?"

She smiled her first real smile since Quinn's arrival. "While I don't appreciate the disparaging marsh-people comment, you're absolutely right. We do love our firearms out here." Her smile faded. "It goes against my nature to claim helpless female, but I really don't want to go into Eddie's room to look for a gun. Would you mind?"

"No problem." He headed into the tiny hall and opened the bedroom door. The tableau inside had turned from dark red to brown already and was beginning to smell. He held his breath as much as he could and performed a quick search. But apparently Eddie wasn't like everyone else out here. There wasn't one single gun to be found. Then again, maybe Quinn had taken Eddie's guns after killing him. Calvin had known Faye would come back here tonight to give Eddie gas money, and Quinn must have forced that information out of him. Poor Eddie. All he'd done was help a friend and he'd paid for it with his life.

Jake returned to the main room and perched on the couch. "Sorry, nothing."

Faye chewed her bottom lip. "I searched the kitchen and under the couch cushions. I even looked in the oven. I suppose he could have a gun in his car. It's worth a look."

"I'll do it. Wait here."

"No. You've got sore ribs and a goose egg on your head. I'll do it."

He blocked her at the door. "I've also got the vest. Unless you want to put it back on?"

She held her hands up in surrender. "You win."

After a quick look out the front blinds, he was reasonably certain they were alone. He hurried out to the carport and searched Eddie's Honda Civic. Nothing. He decided to check the backyard just in case Eddie kept a shed with something useful in it. He grinned when he saw what was sitting behind the house. Finally, something was going their way again.

# Chapter Fourteen

"I can't believe Eddie was so poor and still had this sweet ATV." Jake waited for Faye to slide off the seat behind him before he dismounted.

"I'm not surprised." Faye turned on the flashlight she'd had in her backpack and looked around to get her bearings. The clear sky and bright moon illuminated quite a bit, but it was still treacherous to be this deep in the 'Glades at night, even with a powerful flashlight. She really wished she had her gun and her knife.

"Why aren't you surprised?" He pocketed the keys to the ATV and joined her.

"A lot of people have them around here. It's almost a necessity. I borrow Buddy's ATV sometimes. It's nearly impossible to reach some of the more remote areas without one. It sure saved us a lot of time. We're ahead of schedule."

"Why would you need to go to remote areas out here?"

"Because that's where the most beautiful parts of the Everglades are hidden. There are pristine waterways and saw grass marshes that stretch for miles and miles, untouched by man, just bursting with life. You wouldn't believe the gorgeous flocks of snowy egrets that live out there. Or the incredible plants and flowers. It's breathtaking."

She flushed when she realized he was staring at her. "What? Am I gushing too much?"

He smiled. "Not at all. I enjoy hearing you describe this place. You really love it, don't you?"

"What's not to love?"

"Oh, I can think of a few things. No electricity. No roads. No bathrooms."

"We have all of those back in town, in Mystic Glades."

"Spotty phone service. Internet that fades in and out. Should I continue?"

She gave him an aggravated look and aimed her flashlight off to the right, toward a dark scattering of rocks and downed trees. "That's where we need to go."

"Looks like an obstacle course."

"Yep. We can't use the ATV anymore."

He groaned as if she was taking away his favorite toy. Which, judging from the way he'd grinned when they'd begun their trip, she probably was.

"I don't suppose there's a canal near here. And you've got a canoe hidden away in a strategic spot we could use."

"Uh, no. Fresh out of canals and canoes at the moment. Are you going to start complaining again? I thought I worked those greenhorn complaints out of you when we were looking for Calvin together?"

"Apparently not." He held up a low-hanging branch. "After you."

She murmured her thanks and they started the last long leg of their journey. The terrain here was much rougher than what they'd gone through before. But that's why she'd originally chosen it. She and Calvin had hiked several times through the 'Glades during those summers with Amber, but not through this area. When she'd hidden the journal, she'd wanted to make sure it was somewhere that he'd never been, somewhere he wouldn't think to look.

The path they were following gradually became even rougher as the pines that had outnumbered the cypress trees gave way to almost nothing but cypress. The tree roots bumped up out of the wet ground all around the base of each tree, spreading out for several feet, like knobby knees just waiting to trip her and Jake.

They were forced to slow down and carefully pick their way along the path so they wouldn't fall. They often had to splash through shallow water, or make wide circuits around bogs to find drier land.

Jake glanced up at the dark sky. "These trees are blocking most of the stars. Are you sure we're headed in the right direction?"

"Positive. Everything looks familiar now. We're close."

"How close is close?"

"Maybe another hour."

He groaned. "At least tell me this 'hunting cabin' is kept up and has luxuries like, you know, walls."

She laughed. "Yes, it has walls. And a bed. And a rainwater capture system that filters and supplies water to the kitchenette. It's practically the lap of luxury."

"You didn't mention a bathroom."

"I brought latrine kits."

He shot her a disgruntled look. "Who owns the cabin? I want to complain."

"Buddy."

"Which one?"

She gave him a good-natured shove. "Buddy Johnson, the owner of Swamp Buggy Outfitters. If you're through complaining, we'll be on our way."

An hour later, just as she'd predicted, the cabin she'd told him about came into view. At least, for her it did. She stopped and leaned back against a thick cypress tree.

Jake paused and turned. "Something wrong?"

"Just appreciating how observant you are, Mr. Police Officer Private Investigator Guy."

His hand automatically went to his holster, which of course was empty. He frowned and scanned the woods around them, turning in a full circle. "What do you see?" he whispered.

"The cabin," she whispered back.

He quirked a disbelieving brow and studied the woods again, more slowly. When he saw the structure, he gave her a rueful grin. "You could have mentioned it was camouflaged."

"And spoil my fun? Not a chance." She hurried past him, down the side path that led to the only door. The wood on the little cabin had been painted brown and green to match the trees around it, and nets held dried tree branches against the sides, making it blend in with its surroundings.

She turned the doorknob, but before she could push it open, Jake pulled her back.

"Is it supposed to be unlocked?" he asked, his voice low.

"It's called hospitality. Anyone out this far is welcome to use it. Especially hunters, thus the designation as a 'hunting cabin.'"

He didn't crack a smile at her teasing. "If Buddy wants to help strangers that way, why camouflage the building in the first place?"

"I didn't say it was for *strangers*. Everyone in Mystic Glades knows about this place. If there are any strangers out this far, trust me, they're up to no good."

"Drug runners?" he asked. "I hear they use the Everglades as a drug route."

"So far I've been lucky enough that I've never bumped into any out here. I've heard stories about people using the canals to make their getaway. We've had more than a few meet their end with an alligator or constrictor because they thought jumping into a canal was a good way to escape the cops."

He took her flashlight, gently shoved her behind him and went inside the cabin first, apparently to search for bad guys. She thought the gesture was sweet, but she didn't wait for him to search the place. She could already tell it was empty. It was only one room, with nothing but a full-size bed against the far wall.

Jake frowned, obviously not pleased that she

hadn't waited outside. He stepped past her and bolted the door.

"Mind shining the light over here?" Faye asked.

He pointed the light into the kitchenette. It didn't boast a pantry. There was just a cabinet beneath the sink for things like dishwashing liquid and cleaners and one cabinet attached to the wall next to the door. Inside were a few plates and cups, and two shelves of nonperishable food and some bottled water. It didn't look as if anyone had used the cabin since the last time she'd been here, which meant there was plenty of water and they could snack on crackers and peanut butter. Or she could whip up a can of tuna fish with some of the packets of mayonnaise if Jake wanted some.

"Shouldn't we dig up the journal before we get too comfortable?" he asked.

His bald statement brought the reason for their trip sharply back into focus. She'd been trying not to think about what was at stake while hiking through the marsh. It had been easy since she'd had to concentrate on watching out for predators and trying not to break an ankle by tripping over any downed trees. But now, all of that faded away.

"I'll grab an extra flashlight." She moved a box of saltines to the side and grabbed one of the flashlights from the back. She cracked open a fresh pack of batteries and made sure the flashlight was working before closing the cabinet. "The journal is buried behind the cabin. There should be some tools hanging on the back wall outside, including a shovel. Once we get the journal, I think we should try to get some sleep. The ATV put us way ahead of schedule. And I really don't like being out here at night. We've been lucky so far, but this is hunting time for some of the bigger predators. We can wait here until dawn."

"Works for me. Ready?"

She blew out an unsteady breath. "I guess so. When I buried that thing, I never intended to dig it up again. I'd hoped it wouldn't ever come to that." She pulled back the dead bolt and headed out the door with him beside her.

Jake grabbed the shovel from the back and she led the way between some cypress trees a good thirty feet from the cabin. She stood in the small cleared area and lined up the old, rotted palm that she'd used as a landmark, with the cypress to its right, before pacing off four steps. She used her boot to scrape an X in the soil. "This is it."

Jake broke ground. "How wide and how deep?" He scooped out a shovelful of dirt.

She frowned at how moist it looked. "A foot

wide should do. And only about a foot down. I couldn't go much deeper. The high water table would have flooded the hole."

It took him only a few minutes to widen the hole to the required twelve inches. He scooped out more dirt to deepen the hole. Faye kept her flashlight aimed at the ground where he was digging. He'd gone only half the required depth when his shovel made a sucking sound.

A feeling of dread swept through her. "Please tell me that's not what I think it is."

"Mud." He lifted the shovel out and deposited a gooey, wet pile of dirt beside the hole.

"I chose this place because it's on higher ground and over fifty yards from the nearest bog. It should have been dry." Her fingers curled painfully tight around the flashlight as Jake scooped out two more shovelfuls of mud, the last one so wet that oily black water dripped from it.

His shovel thumped against something hard. He tossed the shovel aside and dropped to his knees to finish digging by hand. Faye helped him, scooping out handfuls of the dripping mud. And she prayed harder than she'd prayed in a long time.

"It's in a plastic bag inside a metal box. It should still be okay. Right?"

Jake glanced at her but didn't say anything.

"I've got it." He cleared mud from the corners of the metal box she'd buried over a year ago. It took some tugging, but the cement-like mixture finally gave up the fight, releasing the box with a giant sucking sound. He wiped the globs of gooey earth away from the top and sides and set the box down in front of Faye. "You do the honors." He held a flashlight and waited.

She hesitated, offering up another quick prayer. Her fingers shaking, she flipped the latch and opened the lid.

"Oh, no." The entire box was filled with the same goo as the hole where it had been buried. "It's in plastic," she repeated. "It will be okay. It has to be." She scooped her hands inside. "I can't find it. It's not here." Panic made her voice a high-pitched squeak.

"Here, let me." He took the box and turned it over, shaking it to let the mud drop to the ground. When the box was empty, he set it aside. He sloughed off layer after layer of mud until, finally, something shiny reflected in the light. He pulled the piece of plastic up, letting the remaining clumps of mud fall to the ground. What once had been a gallon-sized plastic Baggie keeping the journal clean and dry was now bloated and dripping at the seams.

Completely full of mud.

Faye shook her head in horror.

Jake laid the bag on top of the ground and tore it open. The edges of the journal finally came into view. He slid his hand beneath it and picked it up. The pages dropped out in big, wet clumps. Only the leather binding was intact.

"I'm sorry, Faye. Whatever was printed on these pages is gone. The journal is just a soggy mess."

"Gone?" She shook her head. "No, it can't be gone." She pushed his hands aside and feathered her fingers over the top of the mass. She gently tried to peel off what seemed to be a page. It shredded like wet toilet paper. A sob caught in her throat. Her eyes clouded with tears.

"Maybe if we dry it out we'll be able to see something," Jake offered, his voice gentle. "I noticed a small tabletop stove in the kitchenette. We could put a pan on top and set the papers in it, turn the stove on low. When the moisture is out, we might be able to dust off the dirt and still read something."

She latched on to his words like a skydiver desperately deploying the backup shoot when the primary one failed. "Yes, yes, that could work. We'll dry them out." She shoved her flashlight into her pocket and scooped her hands beneath the soggy mess, lifting it free of the mud.

Jake put his hands around her waist and pulled her up. He led her back to the house and inside the kitchen, where she deposited the glob of papers on the counter.

"I'll fill in the hole so no one steps in it and sprains an ankle. Be back in a few."

She nodded, barely noticing the door closing behind him as she grabbed a pan.

JAKE STARTED FILLING in the hole, not that it mattered. It wasn't as if there weren't a thousand other holes out in this wild land just waiting to trap an unsuspecting ankle. But he'd needed an excuse to get away for a few minutes. He couldn't bear to see the despair and hopelessness in Faye's eyes. He'd never met a more capable, strong woman. To see her brought down like this was just…wrong.

And now, with nothing to bargain for her brother's life, and with no weapons, and no way to get help, how was he supposed to protect her? He'd had a vague plan in place when he followed her to Eddie's house. But that plan had mostly consisted of Dex keeping everyone informed—including Deputy Holder, and unfortunately, Quinn Fugate.

Jake had finally admitted to himself last

night at Faye's apartment that he was in over his head out here and needed backup. Dex was supposed to arrange that. But without any way to contact him, even if backup came, they wouldn't know where to go. And what if Quinn saw the police before Jake could get to him? He'd kill Calvin.

Or would he? Jake tried to put himself in the crooked FBI agent's shoes. Quinn was risking everything to find that journal. It must have had some incredibly incriminating entries to justify that risk, something that could put him in prison for a long time, or even send other mob guys after him. Calvin was his leverage to get the journal. So he couldn't afford to kill him and risk Faye giving the journal to the police.

Quinn would have to wait until he saw Faye again before doing anything about Calvin, even if he saw police presence. And if Faye didn't arrive back at Eddie's at the agreed-upon time? Jake shook his head. Quinn still wouldn't kill Calvin. He couldn't lose his only bargaining chip.

With the journal destroyed, the only way to keep Calvin alive was to keep him and Faye apart and hope that Holder showed more interest in the situation than he had at the crash site—because Calvin's survival just might come down to the decisions Deputy Holder made.

Keeping Faye from her brother wasn't a task Jake looked forward to. But hopefully she'd listen to reason and come around to his side of thinking. Either that, or he'd have to trick her.

He smoothed the mud and dirt over the top of the hole and stowed the shovel at the back of the house. He did a quick circuit around the perimeter to make sure there weren't any broken branches or footprints that would indicate Quinn had decided to head into the swamp after all and had somehow followed them. With everything looking okay, he headed inside and locked the door.

When he turned around and saw Faye, he swore beneath his breath. She was sitting in the floor in the middle of the room, a foil pan in front of her with a clump of brown and black inside it. He knew even without asking that the little stove-drying experiment had been a failure. He could tell by the tears coursing down her cheeks.

Faye lifted her head, her expression so bleak it took his breath away. "What am I going to do?" she whispered brokenly.

The desolate look in her eyes, the broken sound of her voice, slammed into him with the force of a hurricane. He'd seen that same desolation in his own eyes when he'd looked in the mirror the day his sister died. He'd choked on those same words, felt the same sense of hopelessness, of loss. The feeling that the world would never be normal again, that he couldn't survive without the one person he cared about the most.

She choked on a sob and covered her face with her hands, leaving muddy tracks down her cheeks.

*Ah, hell.*

He stepped over the pan on the floor and scooped her into his arms.

## Chapter Fifteen

Faye had taken care of Jake, after he was shot. Now it was his turn to take care of her. He set her on the countertop in the kitchenette and gently washed the mud from her hands with a wet washcloth. He washed away every smudge and smear from her tears, every trace of dirt from her face, her arms, her hands, even her legs as she stared off into space. But even though he spoke in low, soothing tones the whole time, trying to get her to react in some way, she acted as if she didn't even know he was there. Tears continued to silently trace down her cheeks.

He rinsed out the washcloth. He'd already washed the mud off himself as well, and there was nothing left to do. She'd refused to drink from the bottle of water he'd offered her, and turned her head when he tried to give her some of the crackers he found in the cabinet.

"I wish I could tell you everything's going to be okay," he said. "But I honestly don't know what's going to happen in the morning. All I can promise is that I'll do everything I can to keep you and your brother safe. Even without the journal. We'll leave early, scout around, come up with a plan long before we get to Eddie's house for the meeting with Quinn."

She blinked and focused on him for the first time since he'd found her staring at the ruined journal, sitting in the middle of the floor. "Why?" she whispered.

He waited but she didn't say anything else. "Why, what?"

"Why would you risk your life to help me? This goes way beyond being hired as a private investigator. I think it's safe to say Quinn's not going to pay your fee anymore." She fingered the silver chain around her neck, something she often did, without even seeming to realize she was doing it.

He grinned. "I suppose it's that whole damsel-in-distress thing. I'm a sucker for a woman in need."

His attempt at humor fell flat. She didn't even smile. What was he supposed to say? Admit that he cared about her? It was crazy to care about someone so fast. He didn't trust it, especially a relationship based on so many lies right from the start, on both sides. Until a few hours ago, he'd thought she was wanted for murder and he was ready to turn her in. And now he knew she was innocent of murder, but she'd stolen that journal. And she was always trying to cover for her brother. For all he knew, she could still be keeping more secrets. He didn't even know if he could trust her. So, why was he helping her? He couldn't answer that. Because he really didn't know.

Since she was still staring at him, waiting, he slid his hand under the necklace to turn her attention. "Are you ever going to tell me what's in that third pouch? The purple one?"

She glanced down and pulled the necklace out from between her breasts. Red, gold and purple pouches hung on the end. She pulled the top of the purple bag open, took his hand and emptied the contents into his palm. It wasn't a bottle with some kind of potion or powder as he'd expected. Instead, it was a pewter figurine, about two inches high.

Both their flashlights were on the countertop, standing on end, pointing up at the ceiling to light the kitchenette. He picked one of them up and shined it on his palm.

"I remember this. It was on your dresser in your bedroom."

"Yes."

"It's a centaur, right? Half man, half horse. Something to do with astrology, I think."

"It's a zodiac symbol. Usually the centaur carries a bow and arrow. Instead, this one is carrying a set of scales."

He turned the little figurine in the light. "Ah, so he is. Like the scales of justice."

"Or scales to balance out the elements, colors, nature...love. That figurine was given to me many years ago, when I had my palm read."

"Read? Like, someone told your future?" He turned the figurine over, impressed with the detail carved into the horse.

"Yes."

At her somber tone, he looked up from the figurine. Her beautiful green eyes captured his. He cleared his throat. "What does the figurine represent then?"

"My fate. The scales and the centaur are linked. One can't exist without the other. The scales are for Libra. The centaur is for Sagittarius."

He grinned. "I'm a Sagittarius."

"And I'm a Libra."

He laughed, but when she didn't laugh with him, he sobered. "Wait? You believe this woo-woo stuff? You think, what, that...you and I...are somehow...fated? What does that even mean?"

She grabbed the figurine and shoved it back into the pouch. "That's the second time you've disparaged my beliefs, and what's important to me." She jumped off the counter and headed toward the bed, her bare feet slapping against the floor, blue skirts fluttering out behind her.

He swore softly. How had she gone from completely nonresponsive to being upset with him in the span of a few minutes? He flicked off one of the flashlights. He brought the other one with him and followed her.

"I wasn't trying to make fun of your…beliefs, or whatever. You kind of threw me with the fate stuff. Are you trying to say something here? About you and me?"

"Not necessarily." She yanked the covers back and slid into bed.

He noted that this time she didn't strip down as she had back in the tent. He sighed and pulled the covers back on his side. When they were both settled, he switched off the flashlight and set it on the floor. He lay on his back, staring up at the dark ceiling.

"What does 'not necessarily' mean?"

She made an aggravated noise and fluffed her pillow. "It means somehow my fate is tied in with the fate of a Sagittarius. Whether it's a good fate or not, I couldn't say. The only thing I'm sure of now is that it's most likely a different Sagittarius than you. Good night." She turned on her side away from him, dismissing him.

He scowled. He didn't believe one bit in her spiritual nonsense. So why did it tick him off that she'd decided *he* wasn't the Sagittarius tied with her fate? He scrubbed his stubble, which was really starting to drive him crazy. He couldn't wait until he was back in civilization again so he could take a real shower and shave.

After several moments of silence, he let out a long breath. Who was he kidding? When this was all over, if they survived, he was going to miss the crazy town of Mystic Glades and all its crazy people. And the person he'd miss most of all was the crazy woman next to him. But she wasn't going to miss him. Of that he was certain. Because once she found out tomorrow that he had no intention of letting her anywhere near Quinn, she was probably going to hate him.

AFTER ONE OF the worst nights of Jake's life, sleeping on a lumpy, far-too-small mattress beside a woman who kept huffing and arching away from him every time he got too close, he was more than happy to see the sun's first rays peeking through the blinds.

Using a latrine kit was just another fun thing

to add to what he was sure would be a miserable day. By the time he and Faye were both ready and had stowed their dirty clothes and toiletries back in their packs, the sun was up enough for them to be able to navigate without the help of flashlights. It was time to go. Thank God.

Faye stood beside him at the door. Her golden hair was captured in a braid for a change, focusing attention on her beautiful eyes, which were as deep green as the bodice-hugging skirt outfit she was wearing. If they were talking right now he'd tell her how gorgeous she was. But so far she hadn't said a word to him, and he refused to be the first one to break the silence. Childish, maybe. But he was in a foul mood and wasn't ready to back down or even apologize at this point.

He grabbed the bolt, ready to slide it back and open the door.

She put her hand on his forearm, stopping him. "Wait. We've been running around so fast getting ready that we haven't even had time to make a plan. How are we going to ransom my brother without the journal?"

They hadn't had time to make a plan because they weren't *talking* to each other, not because they were running around so fast. Then again, since his plan was to keep her going in

circles today and he was going to do everything he could to sabotage their progress, what
was there to discuss?

"We've got several hours of hiking ahead of
us and then a long ride on that cherry ATV. We
can figure out a plan on the way."

She didn't look as if she agreed with him
but she didn't argue. She adjusted one of the
straps on her matching green backpack—which
meant she'd actually unpacked her backpack
from yesterday and had repacked everything
into the new one, all so her outfit would match.
He barely managed to hold back a grin over
that. She squared her shoulders, and her jaw,
as if she were about to march out to face a fir-
ing squad.

She was brave. He'd give her that.

He slid the bolt back and pulled the door
open just a crack to make sure there weren't
any gators, snakes or panthers lying in wait.
The coast was clear, so he shoved the door back
and stepped outside.

Faye closed the door behind her and took the
lead without a word.

They headed down the same path they'd
traveled yesterday, going slowly to avoid the
bumps of cypress roots and soggy marsh encroaching from the woods. So far they'd been
lucky not to encounter any rain, which was

unusual during the summer. But the sky was cloudy today, as if they might get an afternoon thunderstorm or two.

The path wound around a thick clump of trees. A metallic ratcheting sound echoed through the 'Glades.

Jake grabbed Faye to pull her off the path. He jerked to a stop. The muzzle of a rifle was pointing directly at his head from about ten feet away. And the person holding it was Quinn, a cruel smile curving his lips.

"Hello again, Mr. Young. You're looking fit for a dead man. Kevlar?"

He grudgingly nodded.

"Should have thought of that. Take it off."

"What are you doing here?" Faye asked, sounding panicked.

"I thought I'd do you the courtesy of saving you the long trip back. And since I threw a tracking device into your backpack when I searched it last night, it was pretty easy to find you."

Jake swore. Electronic devices never worked for him out here, but of course they'd work perfectly for Quinn. When Faye told him last night that Quinn had searched her pack, he should have thought to look for some kind of tracker. Unfortunately he was still fuzzy from hitting his head and hadn't been thinking clearly.

Quinn waved toward the other side of the path. "I also brought our friend Calvin along to make the exchange easy."

Faye sucked in a keening breath when she saw her brother, a few feet to the right of the path, the white nylon rope wrapped around his waist securing him to a tree. His hands were behind him.

"The vest, Mr. Young."

Jake pulled his shirt off over his head, grimacing when his bruised ribs protested the movement. He tossed his shirt aside and dropped the vest onto the ground.

"Excellent. We're almost done here." Quinn edged over, putting more distance between him and Jake, stopping next to Calvin. He swung the rifle to point at Calvin's head. "Give me the journal, Miss Decker, or your brother dies."

# Chapter Sixteen

"Stop, stop, please," Faye pleaded. "There was an accident. I—"

"Faye, don't," Jake whispered.

"An accident?" Quinn demanded.

Ignoring Jake's warning, she said, "I buried the journal in a metal box, only a foot deep. I thought it would be safe. But the marsh must have crept in during the rains. The journal was ruined. But that's okay, because it means you don't have to worry that someone will see the information. The evidence is gone."

Jake inched closer to Faye, slowly, so as not to draw Quinn's attention. He should have come up with an alternate plan before they left the house, just in case something like this happened. But it was too late. All he could hope now was to try to get Faye to safety before all hell broke loose. He took another step, another...

Quinn's face paled. He shot a quick glance

at Calvin. Calvin narrowed his eyes, his face flushing a bright red. Jake's gaze fell to the ropes around Calvin's waist. Was it his imagination or had they drooped?

Quinn cleared his throat. "What about the account numbers in the journal? There were offshore accounts listed in there. Accounts that can't be touched unless someone knows those numbers."

"I… I didn't know that. This is my fault, not Calvin's. Please don't hurt him."

"Did you make a copy?" Calvin spoke for the first time since the standoff began. His tone wobbled with anger, not fear. Faye must have noticed it as Jake had, because she frowned, her brow wrinkling in confusion.

"No, no I didn't make a copy."

"The money then," Quinn said, sounding nervous. "When your brother took the journal from Genovese's safe, he also took two hundred thousand dollars in cash out of that safe. He said when you two were on the run, you tricked him and stole both the journal and the money. Where's the money now?"

Jake waited for Faye to deny what Quinn was saying. Calvin must have lied to Quinn, to save his own hide somehow, to focus attention on Faye instead. But the miserable look on Faye's face when she glanced at him sent a jolt of dread straight to his stomach. No. No, not possible. She couldn't have stolen that money. There had to be another explanation.

"I don't have it anymore. It's gone," she said.

She didn't have it anymore? Jake clenched his hands into fists beside him. If she had taken that money… No, no, she hadn't taken it. She wasn't that kind of person. He didn't believe it. He *couldn't* believe it.

"It can't be *all* gone," Calvin said.

Quinn glanced at him. If Jake didn't know better, he'd think Quinn looked…scared?

"I'm telling the truth. I don't have the money."

Calvin roared with rage. The ropes binding him fell away. His hands came up from behind him. He was holding a pistol, Jake's pistol. Jake lunged for Faye, throwing her to the ground as the pistol went off. He rolled with her, pulling her behind a tree.

"I need those account numbers, sis!" Calvin yelled. "And I want that money!"

Jake clamped his hand over Faye's mouth when she would have replied. He shook his head in warning and peered around the side of the tree. He jerked back. The bark exploded where his head had been.

Faye's eyes widened. She mumbled something against his hand.

He leaned down and whispered in her ear. "Quinn's dead. Your brother shot him. I think he must have gotten the drop on Quinn before they got here. The rifle had to be empty or Quinn would have fired. And Calvin has my pistol. His ropes weren't really tied. It was all an act. We have to get out of here before he kills us both."

She shook her head in denial and dived away from him. Jake grabbed her, pulling her back behind the tree as the pistol boomed again. She sagged against him, her eyes wide with shock.

"You owe me, Faye! I protected you the whole time we were growing up. You owe me!"

Calvin's wild rantings told Jake just how desperate he was. Which meant he was extremely dangerous. Jake carefully peeked out from behind the tree. His blood ran cold when he realized what was happening. He jerked back behind the cover before anyone saw him, before any of the three men saw him. There were two others with Calvin now. Was that how he'd gotten the drop on Quinn?

Jake sifted through the facts as he knew them. From what Quinn had said, he'd watched Calvin's apartment and grabbed him, and forced him to take him to Faye. That's how they'd ended up waiting at Eddie's, because Calvin knew she was going to return there last night. Maybe some of Calvin's thug friends had seen Quinn grab him. Maybe they'd followed them and after the standoff with Jake and Faye, they'd overpowered Quinn and come up with a new plan. Calvin must have promised them a cut of whatever Faye gave them. Either that's what had happened, or Calvin had somehow planned this all along. Somehow Jake couldn't see Calvin being that smart.

Not that any of that mattered. Not now.

"We have to get out of here. I need you to trust me," he whispered in Faye's ear.

Another bullet cracked into the tree where they were hiding.

She swallowed hard and nodded. He dropped his hand from her mouth.

He looked around, judging the distances from each tree, mentally planning a path that would give them the best cover. He didn't tell her about the other two gunmen. That would only make her more scared than she was right now.

"Okay, we're going to run, fast. Stick with me. Don't stop or slow down to look back. Just do what I do. Got it?"

"Got it," she whispered, her voice breaking.

After picking up a piece of decayed wood lying on the ground, he grabbed her hand and pulled her upright, using the thick cypress as cover.

"Get ready," he whispered. He tightened his hand on hers and threw the wood to the other side of the path. Gunshots echoed through the trees as Calvin and his men fell for the diversion.

Jake yanked Faye's hand and they took off running.

FAYE CROUCHED BEHIND a rotted tree stump, folding her arms in against her body to keep them from showing and making her a target. She couldn't see Jake anymore, or—thank God—Calvin. Jake had learned a lot in the past few days following her as she was tracking Calvin. Now he was off making noises, bending tree branches, doing whatever it took to create a false trail and lead her brother farther and farther away from them. They'd argued before he left, because she wanted to lay the trail. She was afraid he'd end up lost. He'd rolled his eyes and told her he wasn't quite as useless as she thought and had ordered her to stay put. His order rankled. But he hadn't given her a chance to argue.

She slumped farther down, covering her face with her hands. How naive had she been to believe she could change Calvin by taking the journal and the money? Every few months he'd called her about the money, begging her to give it to him, yelling at her, threatening her. But she'd never really thought he would try to hurt her.

The arguments had gotten worse and worse in the past few months. She should have realized how desperate he'd become. He must have gotten himself into trouble with some thugs, or a bookie. She'd always known he didn't have the same values as her, but she never would have expected him to actually kill anyone. And to turn on her—especially over money. He had to be really desperate. That's all she could think. He wasn't himself, wasn't in his right mind.

Some branches clicked together off to her left. She stilled, watching. Jake stepped from behind the tree across from hers, motioning for her to follow him. His gaze darted toward the trees on the other side of her.

She jumped to her feet and ran to him. He grabbed her hand and hauled her close.

"You okay?" he whispered.

"I'm as good as I can be, given the circumstances," she whispered back. "What do we do now?"

"You were a good teacher about the marsh. I followed your instructions and led Calvin off a good ways in the opposite direction and circled back to you. I've found another path, more or less, that will take us toward Mystic Glades, if you're right about the direction you told me."

"I am. I know this area. I know the way back home."

"Okay. Let's go. Lead the way. I wouldn't want to get us lost."

She smiled a sad smile. She appreciated his teasing since she knew he was trying to keep her spirits up. But knowing this particular jaunt through her precious Everglades was because her own brother was trying to kill her...the horror of it was almost beyond what she could handle.

When they reached a small clearing, she pointed to their right, directing him the way they needed to go. He started off ahead of her, as was his habit since this nightmare had begun. If they were going into any trouble, he wanted to be the first one facing danger. Before meeting him, she hadn't even realized men that...good...existed.

Something moved off the side of the path in front of him. She drew in a sharp breath and grabbed his arm.

He stopped and raised a brow in question.

She held her finger to her lips and pointed.

A moment later, an enormous constrictor

slithered across the path right where they would have been if she hadn't stopped him.

"Was that what I think it was?" he whispered.

"Boa. Just like CeeCee."

"Great. Are there very many more of those around here?"

"Probably."

He shuddered, then winked to let her know he was kidding. Her greenhorn was actually getting more comfortable with the critters in the 'Glades. She grinned back at him.

He started to lead the way but again she stopped him.

"What? Another snake?" He studied the path as if a whole family of boas was about to wiggle through.

"No. This is the way I'd normally go to get back to town. But I think we should go back a different way. It won't be as fast. But it might be safer. If we keep heading straight, we'll end up hemmed in by some waterways on one side. Which would be fine if we didn't have to worry about…about my brother. We could get trapped with nowhere to turn. And going into the water to get away is not an option. Trust me on that."

"Alligator snacks?"

"Alligator snacks." She waved her hand to the left. "If we head back that way we can circle around this section of the swamp and get to higher, drier ground. Then we can move back toward town again."

He gave her an admiring look. "You're teaching me to get around in the marsh like a native Mystic Glades guy. And it looks like I'm teaching you to think like a cop. We make a good team. Let's go. I don't know how long my fake trail is going to fool Calvin."

CALVIN WASN'T FOOLED very long at all. Neither were the two men with him. Jake spotted all three of them picking their way through the treacherous boggy soil, driftwood and scrubby pines that dotted this part of the 'Glades, several hundred yards out. The sun had glinted off Calvin's rifle, which he was betting was loaded now. That flash of light on metal had given Jake the warning he needed to throw Faye and himself down behind a fallen tree before they were spotted.

"There are *three* people after us now?" she whispered, her eyes going wide.

"Actually, there've been three after us since the hunting cabin. I didn't want to alarm you. I'd hoped we could outrun them before you found out."

She lightly punched him in the arm. "I'm not a delicate flower. We're a team. Remember?

If we're going to survive we need to communicate better."

"Yes, ma'am. We need to get moving again. Which way?"

She looked around. "Well, we can't cut back toward town the way we were going to go, not without going through Calvin and his men."

"Then we circle around them."

She shook her head. "Can't. This is the only clear area, the highest ground around here. If we go to the left or right of him and those men, we'll end up in gator territory."

Jake peered over the top of the fallen tree again. "Well, we can't stay here. They're heading straight for us. Which means—"

"We head deeper into the 'Glades, and try not to get trapped with the swamp at our backs. Exactly what we were trying not to do." She chewed her bottom lip.

He put his hand on hers. "As long as we watch each other's backs, we've got a chance."

She nodded. They crept toward the trees, staying low so the fallen log would shield them from Calvin's sight.

Another handful of hours found them out of breath and trapped, just as Faye had feared they might be. Jake stood a few feet back from the murky edge of the canal that blocked their way. Behind them, Calvin and his henchmen were still on their trail. Now that Jake knew what to look for, he was able to catch sight of them in the distance every once in a while, and the distance between them was closing. One of the gunmen was obviously a skilled tracker and was able to follow their trail even though both Faye and Jake were doing everything they could not to leave one.

If Jake's guesstimate was right, their pursuers would reach them in about an hour, or less. He stared out over the water, fifty feet across. A quick swim. In and out, just a few minutes, and they'd be on the other side. He scanned the water and the bank on both sides. Not a gator or snake in sight. Just a few egrets and pelicans sunning themselves on the other side of the canal. No ripples in the water to indicate anything sinister lying in wait beneath the surface.

"You sure there are gators in here? Maybe it's the wrong time of day and they're off in their nests somewhere, sleeping."

She snorted. "I grew up in Alabama and I know more about alligators than you do. I thought you were a Florida native?"

"I am. I grew up in a subdivision. By the ocean. The closest I ever get to amphibians is the zoo."

She laughed. "They're reptiles, not amphibians. And trust me. By the time you see them out here in the 'Glades, it's usually too late. The water is *full* of them. And they can hide in the mud so well you might never see them. Don't even think about going in the water."

He glanced nervously at the muddy bank around them, then back at the water. "I'm not sure we have any other options."

"Did you see the movie *Jaws*?"

"Sure. Killer shark. Eats everything in sight."

"No one saw it until it was too late. Picture that waterway full of killer sharks. Do you still want to go for a swim?"

"Okay, okay. We aren't going into the water."

"Maybe I can try reasoning with Calvin. He can't really intend to hurt me. He loves me. Maybe he's just…confused."

"Yeah, shooting Quinn was probably an accident. He *accidentally* pretended to be tied to the tree and *accidentally* shot Quinn in the head. I'm sure he feels awful about it and will be happy to sit and talk with you."

She shot him a glare. "You have a better idea?"

"Plan B."

"Which is?"

"*You* hide and *I* take out the bad guys."

"They have guns. How are you going to take them out without getting shot? Even if you could sneak up within fifty yards of them, that golden tan of yours will make you a gleaming target. And how am I supposed to hide with this?" She flicked her bright green skirts, which swirled in the warm breeze.

"Good point. I don't suppose you'd consider going naked?"

She gave him a droll look.

He grinned. "Didn't think so." He turned around and looked down at the rich, dark mud. Her earlier reference to the movie *Jaws* had other ideas swirling through his head. "Ever see that movie *Predator*, with Arnold Schwarzenegger?"

"Yeah. Why?"

"Plan C."

# Chapter Seventeen

Faye reluctantly handed Jake the veils she'd cut from her skirt. Without the veils, she was left with the lining, which resembled a short, black miniskirt of sorts, barely coming to the tops of her thighs. Thankfully she hadn't gone commando today or Jake would be catching glimpses of a lot more than just her legs while she sat on the muddy bank beside the water.

"You owe me a new skirt," she grumbled. "I still don't know what you want to do with the veils. Or why we're sitting here in the mud."

In answer, he tied the ends of two of the veils together and tugged them tight. "Homemade rope, just in case I get lucky and sneak up on one of those gunmen before he sees me."

She swallowed at his reference to the gunmen, only too aware that they were closing in on them. "And the reason we're in the mud?"

He shoved the veils in his pockets before reaching down and scooping up two large handfuls of the black goo. "You gave me the idea earlier. You said gators can hide in the mud. We're going to cover our bodies with this and blend in with our surroundings, just like in the *Predator* movie." He leaned toward her and slapped the mud on her calves just above her boots.

She stiffened in surprise, but that surprise quickly turned to heat at the feel of his hands sliding over her skin to the sensitive spots behind her knees. When her calves and knees were covered, he grabbed more of the mud, this time dabbing it on more gently and massaging it into her thighs. She should have made him stop. She could certainly put the mud on without his help, but God help her, she couldn't have asked him to stop if a whole posse of gunmen were on their trail. His fingers on her skin felt too good, reminding her of their first meeting, when he'd pinned her to the forest floor. She'd been shocked at her body's answering response to the stranger that night, and had later wondered if she'd imagined the jolt of attraction that had zinged through her core.

Nope. She hadn't imagined it.

The teasing amusement on his face gave way to a taut tension as he continued to rub her legs. His fingers slid higher, higher. She closed her eyes, reveling in the feel of him, waiting, wondering just how high he would go. Wondering just how high she'd *let* him go.

His hands suddenly left her. She barely refrained from voicing her disappointment. He came back with more mud, for her arms this time, and then he moved behind her.

"We can stuff your braid under your shirt, but the gold color still catches the sunlight."

"Go ahead," she said, dreading this part. "You might as wall blot it with mud, too."

He leaned close to her ear. "Sorry about this."

"Me, too."

He rubbed the mud into the blond strands, turning them dark. Then he slid his hands down the back of her neck, and around to the front, stroking her throat. His breath came in short gasps near her ear, and she realized he was just as affected as her.

His hands stilled, and then he was in front of her again. "There, you're effectively camouflaged," he said, his voice tight, husky. "You should put some on your face. I don't want to risk getting it in your eyes."

His Adam's apple bobbed in his throat as she leaned down, purposely allowing her shirt to gap as she scooped up some of the mud. But instead of using it on her face, she dropped to her knees and plopped it onto his bare chest.

He sucked in a breath. "What are you doing?"

"Covering that gorgeous gold skin of yours. If you're going looking for bad guys, you need to blend in with your surroundings, too."

He gave her a tight smile as she slid her hands across his chest, his shoulders. When she trailed her fingers down his abdomen, he sucked in another breath, then coughed as if to cover it up. She moved to his back, only then allowing her smile to escape. She was enjoying this way too much, especially since time was running out. But then again, if this was her last moment on earth, wasn't this the best way to spend it? Enjoying the feel of a warm, sexy man beneath her fingertips?

Yes, that's exactly how she wanted to spend her last moments. She wanted far more than that, but she'd have to settle for what she had time for. She quickly finished his back and his arms, then moved to the front again. She studied him up and down.

"I missed a few spots," she announced. She grabbed two more handfuls of mud then faced him on her knees just inches from his body. She stared up into his eyes as she rested her hands against the golden skin right above the front of his waistband.

His pupils dilated and his gaze dropped right where she wanted it, her lips. She slid her fingers up over the planes of his chest, over his shoulders, to the back of his neck. Then she licked her lips.

That was all the invitation he needed. He dragged her to her feet and then his mouth crashed down on hers, ravishing her, devouring her as one hand cupped the back of her head and the other slid down over the curve of her bottom, pulling her against his hardening length. His tongue swept inside her mouth, teasing, tasting, setting her nerve endings on fire.

He moaned deep in his throat as his fingers slid down, down, kneading her bottom, approaching the very core of her, but stopping just short, with the material of the skirt between his wicked fingers and where she wanted him most.

He suddenly tore his mouth from her and grabbed her shoulders with both hands.

"Don't stop," she breathed.

He shuddered and pressed an achingly quick kiss against her lips. Then he was slapping more mud in her hands.

"This is insane," he said. "We don't have time for this. Hurry up and put the mud on your face. You have to cover all of your skin." He grabbed a handful of mud for himself and scrubbed it onto his face as he ran to the top of the small swell of land, apparently to look for the gunmen.

The sensual haze Faye had been in died a quick death as she stared down at the no-longer-quite-so-appealing mud in her hands. She squeezed the goo through her fingertips in frustration, then closed her eyes and rubbed the mud across her face.

JAKE QUIETLY EDGED through the trees and bushes, careful not to step on any of the dead wood that might snap and announce his presence to one of the gunmen. He still couldn't believe he'd kissed Faye with three gunmen after them. Kissed? Hell. He'd practically consumed her. He'd been one heartbeat away from tearing that erotically tiny miniskirt off her and devouring her right there in the mud. He should have known from experience that the moment he touched her silky legs he would be lost. He should have stopped right then, but his desire to keep touching her was fanned into a wildfire when he felt her pulse leaping beneath his fingertips and knew she was just as turned on as he was. He shook his head, disgusted at himself for losing control when their lives were on the line.

Something snapped in the bushes about twenty feet away. He ducked down, peering through some low-hanging branches and using a tree for cover. He waited and watched, carefully controlling his breathing to make as little noise as possible.

Another snap followed. Leaves crunched beneath someone's foot as the person moved toward him. Branches clacked against each other and leaves lifted as a small branch was shoved out of the way. One of the men who'd been with Calvin stepped into view, his gun in front of him as he scanned the area.

Where was Calvin? And the other man? Had they split up? That would make things easier for Jake, but more dangerous for Faye if the others were out searching for her. He had left her concealed in a hollowed-out tree, bushes tucked in and around her. He'd stood a foot away and tried to see her and couldn't because of how well the mud made her blend in. But what if she made some kind of noise? A cough? A sneeze?

Worry squeezed his chest, but he forced it away. He had to focus on the most immediate threat, the man right in front of him. Twelve feet. Eleven. Ten. Jake timed the man's footfalls, tensing, waiting. The man drew even with the tree where Jake was hiding.

Now!

He jumped up and slammed his foot against

the man's knee and chopped at his Adam's apple at the same time.

The man's scream of pain died in a painful wheeze. He dropped to the ground and clutched his throat. His gun went skittering across the ground, but Jake didn't have to worry that his prey would fight him for it. The man was too busy fighting to breathe through his bruised trachea.

Jake grabbed the gun and checked the loading before sliding it into his holster. Relief surged through him at having a weapon again. He yanked out a length of the green veils from Faye's skirt and dropped down beside the gasping man.

"Stop fighting it," Jake whispered. "You'll be okay if you relax. Hold your breath, then start breathing again, slowly."

The man's eyes widened with alarm when Jake rolled him over and tied his wrists together behind his back. When he was satisfied the man wouldn't be able to break free, he rolled him back over, grabbed the back of the man's shirt, and dragged him to the nearest log.

"Relax, relax, in, out, in, out," Jake coached, hoping he hadn't hit the man harder than he'd planned. He didn't want to kill the guy, even if he deserved it. He secured the man's wrists to one of the thick branches on the log and knelt down in front of him with another wad of cloth from Faye's skirt.

"I'm not going to kill you, all right? Look at me," Jake ordered, keeping his voice low so if the other men were nearby they wouldn't hear him. When the man finally focused on him, Jake nodded. "There you go. You're breathing better. Just relax and the pressure will ease and let more air in." He waited, watching.

The air rattled out of the man's mouth in one last wheeze and settled into a more normal pattern. The panic left his face. Jake waited, holding the wad of cloth. The man suddenly opened his mouth as if to scream. Jake jammed the cloth between his teeth and whipped another veil around the man's mouth, tying it behind his head to keep the gag in.

The man fought the gag, his face turning red. But other than a guttural moan against the cloth, he couldn't scream. His breaths were coming in and out just fine now.

"I'll come back for you, once it's safe." He leaned in close. "Stay alert. I don't think there are any gators in this far from the water, but who knows."

The man's eyes widened and he looked around, as if a gator was about to lunge at him.

Jake grinned and melted back into the trees.

He hadn't been able to resist baiting the man. It was either that or shoot him, and Jake wasn't in the habit of killing unarmed men, no matter how much they deserved it.

He crept through the trees, his gun in front of him as he searched for signs of the other two men.

A gunshot shattered the quiet, sending birds screeching and flying into the sky.

Oh God, no. Faye!

He took off in a sprint, his arms and legs pumping as fast as he could go.

He broke through the trees near where he'd hidden her, pistol drawn.

Half a dozen uniformed Collier County deputies drew on him.

He skidded to a halt, raising his hands in the air.

"Hold your fire!" someone yelled. "That's Young, one of the good guys."

Deputy Holder had yelled that order. The deputies stood down, holstering their weapons. Jake holstered his pistol and ran to Holder, who was supervising another officer handcuffing Calvin's other henchman. Dex had come through after all. He'd sent in the cavalry.

Jake turned in a fast circle, taking inventory. "Where's Gillette? And Miss Star? Did you already take them back to town?"

Holder frowned. "This guy was the only one here when we arrived. We haven't seen Miss Star."

# Chapter Eighteen

A scream sounded from somewhere behind them, followed by a huge splash.

*Oh God, no.*

Jake took off running toward the sounds.

"Wait," Holder yelled. "Remember police procedure, Young. Don't go running in without assessing the situation!"

Jake didn't stop, even when he heard more shouts and people running after him. Holder didn't know what Jake knew. He didn't know about the canal. And the alligators.

*Please let me get to her in time. Please.*

He burst from the trees, onto the muddy bank of the canal, drawing his pistol as he ran. As if in slow motion, his mind's eye saw everything at once—Calvin ripping off Faye's necklace with its gold, red and purple pouches and throwing it into the water; Faye's golden curls flying up as he shoved her under the surface;

two alligators sliding into the canal with barely a ripple, headed straight for Faye and Calvin.

"Let her go," Jake yelled. He aimed his pistol, his finger tensing on the trigger.

Calvin yanked Faye up in front of him, holding her as a shield. Water streamed off her hair like a waterfall. She sputtered and coughed, grabbing Calvin's arm that pressed against her throat.

"Let her go," Jake repeated, entering the water. He kept his pistol in his hand, but pointed it away from Faye. He didn't have a clear shot at Calvin.

"Get out of the water," Holder yelled behind them. "There are two gators coming up fast behind you."

Calvin turned his head, but kept Faye shielding him from Jake's and the officers' guns. "Shoot them," he yelled, his voice sounding panicked. "Shoot them or I swear I'll feed her to them."

"No," Jake yelled. "Holder, don't. You'll hit her. I've got this." He ran farther into the water, off to one side, and shot at the ripples where he thought the gators had gone under. One of them surfaced and hissed but turned back to shore.

"I don't know where the other one is. Calvin, for God's sake, get out of there."

"I'm not going to prison," he yelled, jerking

back and forth, looking for the gator, holding Faye clasped to him in spite of her struggles. "Tell the deputies to back off."

Jake looked at the shore. Five deputies stood on the bank, pointing their pistols at Calvin. Holder stood in the water, not far from Jake, his own pistol down by his side as he watched what was happening.

Something splashed. Jake whirled around. Calvin screamed. A massive alligator broke the surface beside him, its jaws snapping, narrowly missing him. He stumbled backward, pulling Faye between him and the gator.

Jake dived into the water. He surfaced next to Faye. He grabbed Calvin's hand and twisted, hard. A sickening popping noise sounded. Calvin screamed and let Faye go. She dropped into the water. Jake grabbed her and jerked her back just as the gator turned and snapped at her.

She threw her arms around his neck, her eyes wide with terror. Jake ran with her back toward shore, as fast as he could move through the water. Holder met him halfway.

"Take her." Jake thrust her into Holder's arms. He turned and rushed back to shore.

Calvin screamed behind him. Jake turned around and swam toward him as fast as he could go. The gator almost seemed to be playing with Calvin. It circled him, without touching. Then disappeared underwater again.

Calvin sobbed and started swimming toward shore. Jake headed straight for him.

Back on the bank, Faye screamed. "Jake! Look out!"

He dived to the side just as the gator surfaced right where he'd been standing. For the space of a breath, Jake stared right into the cold eyes of the monster. Then it was gone, and Calvin was swimming past him toward shore.

He screamed and went under. Jake treaded the water, shocked at what had just happened. One second Calvin was swimming. The next he was…gone. He shook himself and took a huge lungful of air then submerged beneath the murky surface.

FAYE STOOD BESIDE HOLDER, watching with horror as Jake disappeared. She took off toward the water, or tried to. Holder grabbed her around the waist and pulled her back.

"Don't," he ordered. "He risked his life to save you. Don't throw that away."

"Someone has to help him."

He didn't say anything but he refused to let her go.

She stood there, feeling completely helpless, searching the water's surface, frantically looking for bubbles, something to let her know Jake and Calvin were still alive. What was happening out there under the water?

Suddenly the alligator broke the surface of the water with an enormous splash. Jake was glued to the gator's back, his arms wrapped around its head.

"Oh my God, no!" Faye clapped her hands to her mouth.

Jake clawed at one of the gator's eyes and slammed his fist on the gator's nose. It hissed and rolled onto its back, diving beneath the water again with Jake still hanging on. Bubbles broke the surface. Then...blood.

Faye sank to her knees, horrified sobs escaping from her. "Jake, no, Jake!"

Another splash, a shout. Calvin bobbed to the surface, spitting up water, flailing to keep afloat. And then Jake broke the surface beside him. He grabbed Calvin and turned him on his back, then started for shore.

Faye stared in disbelief. "Where's the gator? Where's the gator?"

Holder pointed. "There, look!"

On the other side of the bank, a gator crawled out of the water, hissing as it headed into the grasses.

Everyone seemed to move at once. They all ran to the water, toward Jake and Calvin, who were in the shallows now. One of the deputies shot his gun into the water behind them, scaring off another hungry reptile, turning it toward the other bank.

Two of the deputies grabbed Calvin and pulled him to shore. His left leg was severely bitten, hemorrhaging blood.

"Get a trauma chopper out here," Holder barked. "Put pressure on that wound."

Faye barely glanced at her brother. She ran straight to Jake and threw her arms around him. "Thank God, thank God, thank God."

He crushed her to him and buried his face against her neck.

JAKE AND DEPUTY HOLDER ducked beneath the MedFlight helicopter's blades and ran to Holder's squad car parked a short distance away in the middle of Mystic Glades's main street. Faye waved from the chopper window as it lifted off, carrying Calvin to Lee Memorial Trauma Center in Fort Myers. The downdraft buffeted the nearby treetops, sending down a rain of oak leaves and pine needles.

When the chopper was just a spec in the sky, Holder motioned to his car. "It's a long drive to the hospital. I wouldn't mind the company. And I'm a good listener. I can have a deputy follow us in your car."

Jake gave him a rueful look. "Is that cop-speak for I'm about to be interrogated and I don't have a choice?"

"Pretty much."

He laughed. "Then I accept your generous offer. Just as long as we stop somewhere along the way so I can get a shirt."

Holder wrinkled his nose. "Trust me. That's the first stop we'll make."

FAYE CLUTCHED HER hands together as she sat in the emergency room waiting area. Calvin had been in surgery for almost an hour. So far, no one had come out to give her any updates. And her only companion was the Collier County deputy standing on the other side of the room who'd accompanied her on the helicopter. She didn't know if he was here to act as Calvin's guard, or hers. Probably both.

Every time the ER doors swooshed open, she looked up, expecting to see Jake. And every time, she was disappointed. Where was he? Shouldn't he have been here by now? He'd said he'd meet her here when Calvin was being loaded onto the MedFlight. There wasn't enough room in the chopper for him to go with her. But he'd had plenty of time to drive here. So why wasn't he here?

The doors opened again. But instead of Jake

walking inside, there were two more Collier County deputies. And they were looking right at her. From the grim looks on their faces as they stopped to talk to the deputy who'd been her shadow for the past couple of hours, she knew she was in trouble.

She turned to the woman next to her, a young, frazzled-looking mother trying to keep her toddler occupied while playing the waiting game.

"Excuse me," Faye said. "I need to call a friend." She pointed to the woman's cell phone sitting on the table between their two chairs. "Would you mind if I borrowed yours? It will just take a minute."

The woman waved toward the table. "No problem, take all the time you need." A delighted squeal had her turning back the other way. "Jimmy, good grief. Get that out of your mouth." She jumped up and ran after her giggling boy, who was now running down the hallway.

Faye picked up the phone and punched in a number. The deputies finished their conversation and the two who'd just arrived moments ago started toward her. Faye clutched the phone. *Hurry up. Pick up, pick up.*

"Swamp Buggy Outfitters," the friendly voice on the line answered.

"Buddy, it's Faye. I need your help. I think I'm about to be arrested."

TURNED OUT, DEPUTY HOLDER had no interest in driving all the way to the hospital. Not after grilling Jake with dozens of questions and deciding he had a whole lot more. He took a detour to the police station and had Jake sit with him in his office to go over everything they'd talked about, again, and to provide a written statement.

"So you don't know for sure whether Quinn or Gillette killed Eddie Stevens?" Holder asked.

"No. He was dead when we got there."

"You and Miss Star arrived separately, though, correct?"

"Yes, and before you go there, she wasn't involved in Eddie's murder. I saw her go into the house and come back out in less than thirty seconds. She didn't have the time, much less motive, to kill him. Besides, the blood was already starting to coagulate when I checked the body."

"Fair enough. Let's circle back to the Genovese murder, in Tuscaloosa. I've been on the phone with the lead detective who worked that case. He confirmed neither Mr. Gillette nor Miss Star...or Decker I suppose...were suspects. There were witnesses who saw both of them at the time of the murder and corroborated their alibis. But he didn't know anything about the journal you told me about."

Jake shrugged. "I would assume that journal was Genovese's secret. It's not likely he would have told anyone about it."

"True. And you told me both Quinn and Gillette were after Miss Star because of the journal. Is that the *only* reason they were after her?"

Jake shifted in his seat. He'd been trying to answer Holder's questions without implicating Faye in the theft of the money. But there was no way he could avoid a direct question without lying. And lying to a fellow police officer wasn't something he was going to do. He let out a deep breath. "No. That's not the only reason."

He filled in the details about the money, about Quinn's claims that there was two hundred thousand in the safe and Calvin's accusations that Faye had taken the money.

"I'm not really sure what to think," Jake said. "Calvin wasn't exactly in his right mind when he said that. He was under some kind of stress and seemed pretty desperate."

"But you said Miss Star told him she didn't have the money anymore. That sounds like she was corroborating his claim that she took it in the first place."

Jake shook his head. "She was trying to placate a man who was shooting at her. Maybe she was worried he'd be even more out of control if she argued that she'd never had the money in the first place."

Holder leaned back in his seat. "Since you're being forthcoming and not lying, I'll go ahead and share what I've learned and try to clear up the confusion over the money for you. Unfortunately for both Miss Star and Mr. Decker, that two hundred grand in Genovese's safe was one of his eccentricities. His financial adviser said Genovese always kept that much in his safe as his emergency fund. When the money wasn't listed in the estate's assets during probate, the lawyer notified the police. They listed it as stolen."

A sick feeling settled in the bottom of Jake's stomach. "You don't have any proof that Faye ended up with any of that money."

"I don't have to prove it. I just have to provide a jury with reasonable doubt. And trust me. That's not going to be hard at all. Did you know that Miss Star had over sixty thousand dollars of student loans after she graduated from the University of Alabama? And that she paid them off a couple of months after

Genovese's death? Tell me, Jake. Where do you think she got that money?"

That sick feeling in his gut became a fiery inferno in his chest. "I have no idea."

"She also started that store, The Moon and Star, not long after Genovese died. Any idea where she got the money for the inventory?"

Jake slowly shook his head. "No."

A knock on Holder's open door had him glancing up in question at the police officer standing there.

"They're ready for you, sir."

"Thanks." Holder shoved his chair back from his desk. "Looks like we're about to get our answers. You're welcome to watch with me if you want."

Jake stood. "Watch what?"

"Miss Star's interview on the closed-circuit monitor. They just brought her in. Detective Davey is interviewing her right now."

By the time the interview was over, Jake felt raw, as if someone had ripped his heart out through his throat and stomped on it. Faye had looked so innocent. She'd sounded so convincing—her tone at least. But her excuses sounded anything but convincing.

*I don't know who paid off my student loans. Freddie Callahan bought the inventory for the store. I didn't have much money when I came to Mystic Glades.*

*No, I didn't take the two hundred thousand dollars from the safe. Calvin did.*

*Yes, I took the money from Calvin, but only because he shouldn't have taken it in the first place. I don't have it anymore. No, I didn't spend it. I donated it to charity. I saw on the news which charity Mr. Genovese's estate had donated everything to so I sent the money to the same one, just like the lawyers would have done if Calvin had never taken the money.*

*No, of course I don't have a receipt. It was an anonymous donation.*

Jake had heard enough. He was disgusted with himself for trusting Faye, and for letting himself fall for her. Because there was no question any more that he *had* fallen for her. Only a lovesick fool would have believed the lies she'd told him, especially with his background as a police detective. He should have known better. He did know better. But he'd closed his eyes to all the signs that pointed to her guilt. He'd convinced himself it was all Gillette, when Faye was just as guilty as her brother.

The door on the interview room opened and Detective Davey stepped out, pulling a hand-cuffed Faye along with him to be processed into the jail.

Her eyes widened when she saw Jake sitting at the desk a few feet away with Holder.

"Jake," she called out. "They're arresting me. Help me. I don't know what to do."

He steeled himself against the panic in her voice. She was a liar, a thief, a criminal. And so damn beautiful it almost hurt to look at her. But he'd never be fooled by that beautiful shell again. Because the woman inside was ugly.

Her brows creased with confusion. "Jake?"

He stood and walked out of the squad room without looking back.

JAKE STOOD IN front of his bathroom mirror and studied his reflection. Freshly showered, freshly shaved, dressed in a clean pair of jeans with his shirt tucked in, he should have felt like a new man. Especially after spending most of the past week hiking through mud and swamps. Instead, he felt empty. Drained.

And guilty as hell.

He kept hearing Faye's voice. Not when she'd asked him for help, but when she'd called out his name. Just one word, four letters, but they'd carried so much fear, pain and ultimately confusion as she realized he wasn't going to help her.

Had he done the right thing? He didn't have a clue. His life had been black-and-white before this case. The lines between good and bad were clear, solid, easy to separate. Now? Now everything was murky and gray. Because even though Faye had lied, so many times, and she'd broken the law, he was making excuses for her. And he was doing everything he could to keep himself busy so he wouldn't jump in his car and drive back to the station and beg for her forgiveness.

His phone rang, the landline in the kitchen, which was the only way anyone could get in touch with him now that Quinn had destroyed his cell phone. He'd have to remember to pick up a new one. Maybe tomorrow. Because tonight he was pretty sure he was going to end up too drunk to go anywhere.

He grabbed the phone on the second ring. "Young."

"Would it have killed you to call your business partner and friend to let me know you're alive?"

He plopped down in one of the chairs at the kitchen table. "Dex. Sorry. So much has been going on. You're right. I should have called."

"You sound like hell."

"I feel like hell."

"Well, maybe this will make you feel better. When you didn't call—after I went to all that trouble to convince Holder to go to Mystic

Glades and look for you and save your sorry butt, I might add—I called him for an update. He brought me up to speed. He told me the charges against Faye were dropped."

Jake straightened in his chair. "What? What are you talking about? When did you talk to him?"

"About five minutes ago. Seems that her claim about donating the two hundred grand has been corroborated by the charity. They pulled their records and confirmed the donation was made when Faye said it was, and that it was made in Genovese's name. The Tuscaloosa police were more than happy not to pursue charges. With Quinn as their guy for Genovese's murder, they can close that case and move on."

"But…what about the student loans? Faye paid off sixty thousand dollars' worth, right after that money was taken from the safe."

"No, *Freddie Callahan* paid off Faye's student loans. Some guy named Buddy drove Freddie to the station with a receipt for the payment to prove it. Apparently Freddie thinks of Faye as a daughter and didn't want her to worry about her debts. But she didn't want Faye to feel beholden to her, so she paid the loans anonymously. She's innocent. All charges dropped. She's on her way back to Mystic Glades right now."

Jake groaned and dropped his forehead against the table.

"Jake? This is a good thing, right? Jake?"

"I'm such an idiot. I totally screwed up. I thought she was guilty."

"We both did. No big deal. Wait. Why does it matter?"

Jake didn't say anything.

"Um, okay," Dex said. "I'm guessing there's a whole lot more to your little trip through the Everglades than you've told me. And I'm also guessing we care what Miss Star thinks now?"

Jake forced himself to sit up. "Yes. No." He cursed viciously.

"All righty then. I'm going to hang up. Call me back when you're in a better mood."

Jake clutched the phone. "I did her wrong, Dex. I hurt her. I don't expect she'll ever be able to forgive me. I don't even want her to. I don't deserve it. I didn't believe in her. But I should have."

"Well, then maybe you need to show her you believe in her now."

"Yeah, right. It's a little late for that. How am I supposed to do that? I didn't believe she was innocent. I didn't believe in *her*, or even what was important to her. I've mocked her belief system more than once. I called it woo-woo science. At least twice."

"Ouch. You're toast."

"Pretty much. I just wish there was something I could do to make it up to her. She's lost her brother. He's going to prison for a long time. And she's been alone most of her life. She even had this crazy idea about her future, a plan, all because of some fortune-teller." He stiffened. "Wait. That's it. That's what I can do to make it up to her. I can give her back her future, her dreams."

"Uh, hey, pal. I think you might have been hitting the bottle a bit early today."

"Nope. Haven't had a drop. You have that fancy computer of yours handy?"

"Always. Why?"

"I need to you to surf the net for me."

## Chapter Nineteen

Jake drove past the alligator sign that announced the entrance to Mystic Glades and drove under the arch.

*Bam!* Something exploded against his window. He slammed on his brakes. *Bam! Bam!* Two more missiles exploded against the glass, spilling their slimy, yellow goo.

Eggs. Someone was pelting his car with eggs. Awesome.

He turned the windshield washer on and continued down the street. More eggs slammed against the windshield, the roof, his door. But whoever the culprits were, they were hiding so well he hadn't seen any of them. He continued his drive of shame down the street, past The Moon and Star, and parked in front of Swamp Buggy Outfitters.

He got out of the car with the tool he'd bought after Dex had located a store for him. *Bam!* An egg slammed against the side of his head. He clenched his jaw and ignored the sticky slime as it dribbled down his jaw. He marched into SBO.

Buddy was sitting with the other old-timers by a display of canoes. His gaze shot to the egg dripping from Jake's hair as Jake strode toward him. Buddy stood, his jaw tight when Jake stopped right in front of him.

"Buddy, I need to borrow your swamp buggy."

*Bam!* White-hot fire burst inside Jake's skull as he flew backward from the force of Buddy's punch. He landed on a display of beanbag chairs that thankfully softened his fall. He held his hand to his throbbing cheek and pushed himself upright just as Buddy and his crew circled around him like a pack of vultures ready to pick his bones, except they weren't willing to wait until he was dead before starting their meal.

Buddy drew back his fist again.

Jake held his hands up in surrender. "I deserved that. I deserved that and a whole lot more. And if you want to beat me to a pulp I'll let you, but not right now. I have something more important to do. And I need your help."

Buddy bobbed on his feet like a championship boxer waiting for an opening. "And why would I want to help a slimeball like you?"

"Because I'm not asking you to help me. I'm asking you to help Faye."

He slowly lowered his fists and gave him a suspicious look. "Start talking."

FAYE STOOD BESIDE Amy and Freddie looking out the front window of her shop toward SBO.

"What do you think he's doing in there?" Amy asked. "And what was it he carried in there? It looked like a cattle prod or something."

Faye shook her head. "I have no idea." She chewed her bottom lip. "He's been in there a while. I hope he's okay."

Freddie snorted beside her. "Quit worrying about him. Whatever happens, he's probably getting what he deserves. And we certainly don't care." She grabbed Faye's shoulders and pulled her away from the window.

"Wait," Amy called out. "That huge glass window is opening up like a door on the front of the store." She pressed her hand to her chest. "Oh, my gosh. What are they doing?"

Faye and Freddie hurried back to the window. Buddy's brand-new, state-of-the-art swamp buggy rolled through the enormous door out onto the street. Buddy was driving. At least a dozen of his friends were sitting on top of the platform with him. And standing beside Buddy was Jake, holding that crazy-looking pole contraption he'd had when he got out of the car.

The buggy turned and headed down the street, toward the swamp.

"What in the world are they doing?" Amy cried.

Freddie pulled Faye back from the window again. "Like I already said, we don't care. Faye, you said you'd make up a batch of that hand lotion for my friend, Estelle. Well, time's a wastin' and she's not getting any younger."

Faye let her friend lead her to the counter. There was no point in staring after Jake anyway. He'd made his feelings for her—or lack of them—perfectly clear when he'd abandoned her at the police station.

FAYE PATTED ESTELLE'S HAND. "Just put the lotion on twice a day and your hands will be soft and smooth again in no time."

"Thanks, Faye. You're the best." Estelle gave her a hug and headed out of the shop.

Faye slumped against the counter. "Let's close up early tonight, Amy. I'm worn-out. I don't know what I was thinking opening today anyway. We'll just have to work extra hard this weekend to make up for the lost sales."

"You're the boss." Amy straightened one

last row of jewelry in the window display and turned to go. "Faye, wait, wait! They're back. And they're coming this way!"

Faye hurried in from the back room. "Who's back? What are you talking about?"

"The guys. Buddy and..." She bit her lip. "Jake."

The door to the store burst open. Jake stood in the opening, covered from head to toe in dirt and mud. He glanced at Amy and looked around until he saw Faye standing in the hallway. He marched toward her, and behind him Buddy and all of his friends poured inside. They were all grinning and holding rifles. Everyone except Jake.

Faye put her hands on her hips. "Buddy, what did you guys do to him?"

"Nothing, honest." He coughed. "I may have punched him, but that was before."

"Before?" She blinked and looked up at Jake, who had stopped right in front of her.

"Faye."

"Jake." A big glob of mud slid down from his hair and plopped onto the carpet. She winced. That was going to stain.

"I was a jerk."

She looked up at him. "Uh, yeah. You were. What did you and Buddy—"

"I didn't believe you. I should have. I'm sorry."

She leaned over and peered behind him. The entire shop was filling up. Freddie was back, leaning against a display, drinking from a bottle of Hennessey, or whatever homemade brew she'd put in the bottle. Sammie gave her a sheepish wave from the corner by the clothing racks, with CeeCee draped over his shoulders. She straightened and cleared her throat. "So that's why you're here? To apologize?"

"Yes. I mean, no. I came here to give you this." He grabbed one of her hands and covered it with one of his own.

She felt something cold and hard in her palm. He closed her fingers around it.

"I really am sorry. And I'm probably half in love with you. I don't know. All I know for sure is that you deserve better than the way I treated you. I should have respected your beliefs, respected you, believed in you." He leaned in and kissed her cheek. He squeezed her hand in his. "I hope you find the right Sagittarius one day."

He turned around and walked out of the store.

Faye uncurled her fingers and looked down at what lay in her palm. The centaur, holding up the set of scales. The same one Calvin had tossed into the swamp. She blinked at it in confusion.

"He dove into that alligator-clogged cesspit to find that for you." Buddy stood in front of her now. He pointed at the figurine. "He had some fancy-shmancy underwater metal detector. Had all of us stand on the bank and shoot the water to scare the gators away so he could keep diving until he found that. Even so, there were a couple of close calls. Had to drag him out a couple of times or he'd have sacrificed himself to the alligators for you. But he wouldn't quit, wouldn't stop going back in the water until he found that. I don't know what that little figurine means to you, but apparently he thought it meant enough to you to risk his life for it." He cocked a brow. "So what are you going to do about that?"

The other old-timers gathered around him in a circle, grumbling and adding "yeah, yeah" on top of Buddy's statement, as if suddenly she'd become the bad guy in this scenario.

Freddie sidled up to her and put her arm around her shoulders. She dabbed at her eyes and sniffed. "Well? Don't just stand there. Go get him."

Faye handed the figurine to Freddie and ran to the front window. She had to push half the townspeople aside to look out at the street.

"His car is gone! He already left."

"Faye, catch," Buddy called out.

She turned around and caught the keys he threw to her. "Thanks, Buddy!"

"Don't thank me. Just hurry."

She turned and ran out the front door.

HE SHOULD HAVE washed the egg off his car somehow before he'd left Mystic Glades. Jake punched the windshield washer button again. Half the fluid shot up on top of the roof instead of on the windshield, rewetting the egg that had already dried and making it slide down onto the windows. He shook his head in disgust.

Something black ran across the road in front of him. He swerved to avoid it, sliding sideways to a bumpy stop. *Sampson.* The panther stopped at the edge of the trees and looked back. If Jake didn't know better, he'd swear the panther was grinning at him. It disappeared into the swamp and Jake took off again. He rounded the next curve. His eyes widened and he slammed on his brakes again.

When his car shuddered to a complete stop, he sat there staring in disbelief at what was sitting in the middle of the road: Buddy's swamp buggy, squatting like a World War II tank ready to take out anything that tried to pass. And standing in front of it, pointing a rifle at him—as usual—was Faye.

Great. Just great. He shoved the door open. Just as he was getting out, a gooey piece of egg slid off the roof onto his head.

*Wonderful.*

He sloughed it off, shook his head and shuffled reluctantly to confront the little armed pixie waiting for him. She tossed the rifle down when he reached her.

"You have egg on your face," she said.

He sighed. "Yes. I know. I admit it. I screwed up. I'm a jerk. A slimeball. Or the worst insult Buddy could think of this afternoon, a 'city slicker.' I'm in total agreement with all of the above."

Her brows creased. "What? Oh. No, no, no. I mean, *literally*. You have egg on your face. You… Here. Just, let me…" She reached up and wiped his face. A glob of yellow fell to the road.

"Perfect," he mumbled. "Anything else?"

"Just this." She put her arms around his neck and jumped up, wrapping her legs around his waist.

He stumbled back against his car with her in his arms and plopped down on the hood. "Um, okay, what, *ergmgf*—"

She covered his mouth with hers and scorched him with a searing kiss. When she pulled back, all he could do was wait for the punch line. Because *this* was not what he'd expected.

"Say something," she said.

"I... I don't even know where to begin. I thought you were going to shoot me, not kiss me. I'm getting mixed signals here."

She lightly punched him in the arm. "Are all city slickers this slow? Don't you get it? You were wrong, back at the store."

Now, this was what he'd expected. "I know. I'm sorry."

She rolled her eyes. "You were wrong because you think I still need to find my Sagittarius. Jake, I don't need to search anymore. I've already found my perfect Sagittarius, my fate, my future. You."

He blinked, certain he couldn't be hearing her right. "But I was terrible to you. I didn't believe in you. I left you."

"Oh come on. Seriously? Even if you're a PI, you're still a cop. You have standards. You thought I was a criminal. Did you hurt me by walking out? Yes. But I understood why you did it." She kissed the tip of his nose. "You're spiritually challenged."

"Spiritually...what?"

"You don't understand fate the way I do. And it's only been a few days. You need time to come to grips with everything, to understand that you and I are meant to be together. It's okay. You've come a long way in a short amount of time. I'll be here to teach you what you need to know. I'll be patient with you."

"Faye, sweetheart. I have no idea what you're saying. But I hope what you mean is that you forgive me."

She punched his arm again, a little harder this time.

He winced.

"Of course I forgive you," she said, smiling.

He swallowed hard. "Okay. And the rest of what you said, it means...you're not going to shoot me?"

She let out a big sigh. "It means, *sweetheart*, that it's time for plan D."

He frowned. "Plan D?"

She curled her fingers into the front of his shirt, all signs of humor gone, her emerald green eyes searching his. "That's the part where you fall in love with me."

He stared at her in wonder, stunned at his good fortune, at the amazing, incredible woman who had burst into his life. And completely undone by the love shining in her eyes. For him. In spite of all his faults, in spite of all the mistakes he'd made, she loved him. And all she asked in return was that he fall in love with her.

His hands shook as he cupped her face in his palms. "Too late," he whispered, "I already did that." He covered her mouth with his.

\* \* \* \* \*

*Look for more books in Lena Diaz's*
MARSHLAND JUSTICE *miniseries*
*in 2016!*
*You'll find them wherever*
*Harlequin Intrigue books and*
*ebooks are sold!*